A DUBIOUS PROSPECT

ANNE CLEELAND

OTHER REGENCY ADVENTURES BY ANNE CLEELAND

Tainted Angel
Daughter of the God-King
The Bengal Bridegift
The Barbary Mark
The Spanish Mask
The True Pretender
A Death in Sheffield
The Gypsy Queen
The Blighted Bride
The Stray Relation

For James' mom, who won the battle; and for all the others who didn't, may they rest in peace.

CHAPTER 1

*R*obert Tremaine, late of His Majesty's diplomatic service, contemplated the task ahead of him as his horse picked its way up the rocky pathway. He was headed up to a mountain homestead that he'd visited once before, here in south of Spain—a homestead for which he now held a farming license.

He'd been posted here during the Peninsular War, on assignment to monitor the previous owner of the property—a Spaniard named Tosada, who lived at the homestead along with his wife. At that time, Tremaine was an operative for the shadowy forces that worked behind the scenes during the war, and his spymaster had asked him to monitor this remote homestead on the belief that weapons and ammunition were being delivered to Napoleon's forces covertly, through the pass at the peak of the mountain.

At the time, Napoleon's march through Europe had been severely hampered by the massive problems the Spanish *guerrillas* were creating for Napoleon's supply trains—wagons full of ammunition and weapons that were heading toward the front. The *guerrillas* were an irregular group of Spanish civilians—ferocious and loyal to Spain—who'd used stealth and sabotage to wreak havoc upon the supply trains as they progressed along the major roads. It was an amazing turn of events, that a small band of determined men—who paid little attention to the usual rules of warfare—could have such a profound effect on the Emperor's plans for conquest.

As a result, his forces had started avoiding the main routes to deliver war supplies, and had instead used different, less obvious alternatives—one of them being this mountain pass.

As part of his assignment, Tremaine had duly reported that supplies were indeed being ferried by horseback over the mountain pass, and that the homestead near the peak of the mountain was being used as a way-station for the riders. Since French soldiers could not openly attempt this supply route without fear of discovery, Spanish *Afrancesados*—those Spaniards who'd pledged loyalty to Napoleon

—were being used as the carriers. A steady stream of them were coming up the mountain—traveling quietly, and at dusk—and then the next morning the riders would embark on the journey over the pass, their horses laden with as much as they could carry.

It was an extremely inefficient way to deliver weapons and ammunition, and so it meant that there wasn't much to show for the hard climb over the mountain; obviously, the *guerrillas'* tactics had forced Napoleon's generals to take rather desperate measures. And that very inefficiency was probably why Tremaine's commander had been content merely to monitor the situation, and had not asked him to perform any acts of sabotage during his time here; much of war-strategy was in knowing when to allow the enemy to make mistakes.

Therefore, the time Tremaine had spent monitoring the homestead had been tedious and uneventful, but he'd enjoyed it nonetheless; it was a welcome respite from the horrors of war and he'd felt a sense of peace, there in the clear, crisp mountain air—there was nothing like a mountain sky, to take one's mind off one's troubles. The area rather reminded him of his home in Wales—quite the surprise, that he'd be nostalgic about it—and so he'd done a bit of exploring, covertly climbing about in the crags that surrounded the homestead's meadow, reminded of happier times when he'd done the same as a lad. And it was in doing that exploration that he'd made a surprising discovery—a discovery that had led him to his return to this mountain, four years later.

Of course, much had changed, since then. Napoleon had been captured—and was now a prisoner on the Island of Elba—which meant that at present, there was a tentative peace in this area of the world; much appreciated, after eight long years of war. But the peace was indeed only tentative; Napoleon might be in exile, but the people who knew about such things seemed to think it was only a temporary setback, and that he'd soon attempt another conquest of Europe. It didn't help matters, of course, that the forces who'd supported him were emboldened by the current chaotic weakness on display, as the beleaguered nations of Europe met in Vienna in an attempt to piece themselves back together again.

And this threatened follow-up to the last war was a source of immense frustration for Tremaine, being as he was no longer a member of the diplomatic service—no longer in a position to help his country, and make use of his well-honed skills.

He was no longer in the service because he'd mucked things up a bit, and as a result had been discharged—a run of bad luck, mostly. But he'd make things right—was bound and determined to redeem himself, and return to his former role—and he'd hit upon a possible means to do it, so long as his suppositions were correct. He'd wager he had the right of it, though—it was luck beyond measure that he'd once been assigned to this remote, mountainous place to keep watch, and that he happened to have a background in mining. It would serve him well, hopefully; he was in dire need of a bit of luck, just now.

He paused to allow his horse to rest—it was a steep climb, and old fellow was winded but he was the best Tremaine could afford with what was left in his purse.

Squinting at the rocky terrain with a practiced eye, he contemplated the remainder of his journey. Wales had nothing like these mountains, of course, but mountains were all made the same way—no matter their size—and what they held within them could be predicted, if one had a practiced eye. When he'd last explored the rocky crags around the homestead, he'd noted several tell-tale signs that would indicate the area was rich with ore—even the surface veins seemed fairly obvious. And he wouldn't be surprised—God willing—if a goodly portion of that ore was gold.

He was aware that other parts of this mountain range had been mined since the Romans, but it didn't look as though anyone had done much mining on this particular mountain; a practiced eye could recognize the signs, even hundreds of years later. In particular, it didn't look to him as though anyone had attempted to mine the stream that meandered down from the peaks—no one had set-up a dam, anywhere along its length.

And so, he'd made a mental note of it, back then; perhaps he'd try to return here after the war, to find out whether his hunch was correct. Little did he know that his hunch would one day serve as his best chance at redemption—an opportunity to set everything to rights, and get his proper life back again. His Majesty's service may have washed their hands of him, but he'd been given a chance to turn it all around because he'd noticed something that no one else had; that this remote mountain pass could wield a fortune to the right man.

Therefore, he'd sold his horse and—together with his pension-money—had managed to buy a farming license in the property; he couldn't afford to buy the property outright, because he'd never been able to save much money, unfortunately. And so, he'd bet his entire future on this gamble, and was determined that it would pay off—determined that he would redeem himself, and rejoin his former colleagues in fighting the good fight.

As the horse picked its way forward again, Tremaine mentally winced a bit, thinking about them. He'd shared more than few adventures with some very brave people during the war, and until he righted his ship he didn't know how he could ever face any of them again. A few had reached out to him—offered him a place to stay, until he'd found his feet again—but he too ashamed to face them. That, and he was not keen on allowing anyone to look too closely into his private habits.

Reaching to pull the whiskey bottle out of his saddlebag, he took a long pull—his current, rather bleak situation brought to mind his family back in Wales, but he didn't want to think about them, just now. They'd been miners for generations, but he'd never got on with his father—who was something of a brute—and so he'd decided early-on that he would escape as soon as he was able, and he'd left them all behind with nary a backward glance. He'd die here in the Spanish hills before he'd ever go back with his tail between his legs, so best to put them out of his mind and concentrate on the task ahead.

Wiping his mouth with a sleeve, he returned the bottle to the saddlebag and hoped he'd enough whiskey to last a few days, until he could return back down the mountain to the town that stood at its foot. He'd no money, but with any luck he'd find something to barter at Tosada's old homestead—perhaps a blanket, or a cooking pot. And if everything had already been picked clean, he could always trade game for whiskey—during the war, he'd become proficient at living off the countryside, hunting birds and rabbits.

He urged the horse onward, and the rest of the journey passed uneventfully—indeed, he truly couldn't remember much of it—and then he finally arrived at the high meadow that held the old homestead.

He paused for a moment, looking it over in the fading sunlight; nothing seemed to have changed since last he was here, and blowing-out a long breath of relief, he felt a flicker of optimism. It was a pretty sight, this time of year—the sky was clear blue, the grass was dark green and you could hear the soothing sounds of the stream that ran through the high meadow—the wellspring was somewhere up high in the rocky crags. Hopefully, that same stream was bringing gold along, as it wound its way down from the higher elevations—and with that gold, his salvation.

The homestead itself was old and battered—a two-room shack, with a separate, makeshift barn—very similar to the shelters that lined the Welsh valleys, where the shepherds had worked their sheep. The place would need a bit of work, of course, if he was going to survive the next winter and set-up a mining operation, but he'd never been afraid of a bit of hard work. With a renewed sense of purpose, he urged the horse forward; things were finally going to turn around—he could feel it.

Recognizing the end of the journey, the tired animal picked up his pace as they approached the building, and then his long ears twitched forward, as though he were listening.

Abruptly, Tremaine pulled to a halt, swearing to himself. He was losing his touch, if he hadn't thought to reconnoiter first; it was entirely possible there were squatters or even outlaws within the structure—it was far up in the mountains, and would make a good hiding place.

"Ho," he called out, his hand resting on his pistol. "Is anyone within?"

To his surprise, the door began to open slowly, and he quickly slid off the saddle to stand behind his horse, propping his pistol atop the saddle and aiming it toward the door. After a tense moment, he ran a hand over his eyes—trying to focus—because he almost couldn't believe what he was seeing; within the doorway stood a young woman—a young woman who was leveling a musket at him.

"Stop," she called out in Spanish. "Come no closer."

Listening intently, he took a quick glance around. "Are you alone?"

Narrowing her eyes, she cocked her head. "Are *you* alone?"

"Yes," he admitted. "Who are you?"

"I own this property. Who are you?"

With some surprise, he stared at her for a moment, trying to gather his wits. "I was told the owner lived in Madrid."

"My husband was the owner, but now he is dead."

So, he thought, trying to make sense of it even though his mind wasn't very clear; this must be Tosada's wife. He'd caught a few glimpses of her when he'd been here before, but he hadn't paid much attention, since she tended to remain in the homestead whilst the men conducted their covert operations. It had never occurred to him that she might still be here, and he managed, "I am—I am sorry for your loss, Señora. My condolences."

"Who are you?" she repeated, unfazed.

"My name is Robert Tremaine, and I hold a farming license for this land. I bought it from the mercantile agent in San Ysidro."

She frowned in suspicion; the muzzle of the musket unwavering. "How can this be?"

"I don't know," he admitted, as he decided to sheathe his pistol. "Do you mind if I come in?"

"I believe you are drunk," she accused.

Very much on his dignity, Tremaine replied, "I am not drunk, but I certainly didn't expect you to be here."

"I did not expect you to be here, either."

He blew out a breath, and held out his hands, showing his palms. "Do you mind if I come in, so that we can sort this out?"

"My brothers will be back soon," she warned.

With a small smile, he assured her, "I'm not going to hurt you—I promise. But it's coming dark, and my horse needs to be rubbed down, poor fellow."

Coming to a decision, she lowered the musket. "Very well. You can sleep in the barn, with my donkey."

Tremaine chuckled as he steadied himself against his horse. "Gladly. I hope your donkey doesn't snore."

"He must hope that you don't," she returned rather tartly.

CHAPTER 2

Tremaine woke the next morning feeling a bit groggy, and it took him a minute to remember where he was—until the scent of the donkey and the sound of chickens brought it all back to him.

Last night, the widow had given him a blanket and a few biscuits, and then he'd retreated to the barn to see to his horse, and prepare a makeshift bed in the hay rack. It was no hardship—he'd spent many a night in similar circumstances during the war—but on the other hand, he hadn't spent his last farthing to sleep in a hay rack, and so he'd best straighten-out whatever misunderstanding had brought him to this awkward situation. Either the young woman was lying about owning the land—it was a possibility; he'd run across many a glib female who would take whatever advantage she could—or the mercantile agent in the town had cheated him. And cheated her, too; it remained to be seen.

As though on cue, he could hear the woman's voice, calling from without. "Are you awake? I have coffee."

Shaking his head to clear it, he stood and opened the door to see that she was holding a tin coffee-pot and regarding him rather warily. He'd already decided she was a foreigner—her Spanish had a rather clipped accent that he didn't recognize, which was interesting because he'd become adept at sorting-out such things during the war. She had olive-toned skin, and was dressed in peasant's garb—a simple blouse and a skirt that fell to her calves, with her hair bound-up in a linen scarf.

He gauged that she was late twenties or early thirties and all in all, seemed non-threatening—although obviously she was no soft miss, if she'd been helping Tosada with his operation; best be on his guard.

"Thank you," he said, mustering-up a disarming smile. "Please come in."

She walked past him, and he decided that she was rather striking; she was tall—nearly as tall as he—and there were tendrils of honey-colored hair that had escaped her scarf—hair that almost matched her light brown eyes. Her hands were long and thin—as were her legs—and her legs seemed long, in proportion to her torso. A desert-dweller from North Africa, he guessed, and wondered how she came to be here.

"I have a pistol," she warned, because indeed she did—incongruous in a leather holster, slung over her apron.

He already knew from last evening that she was comfortable with a firearm, and so he readily offered, "I mean no harm—I promise—but there seems to have been some sort of misunderstanding."

She turned around to face him, leaning against the hay rack and knitting her brow as she studied him. "You are not English," she observed.

"And you are not Spanish," he replied.

She smiled slightly. "My name is Mora. I am from Morocco."

This affirmed what he'd guessed, and he asked, "You were a slave?" Spain had abolished slavery only a few years before, and many former slaves had stayed in the country rather than make the trip back to their homeland.

"No, but very close to it. My father contracted to marry me to a man he owed money to."

He nodded, since this was the way of it, in many places of the world. A man viewed his children—especially his daughters—as property to be bartered or sold as he saw fit. But it seemed to him that Mora's arranged marriage to Tosada had not hurt her—she seemed fit and healthy, and she didn't have that browbeaten attitude you tended to find when dealing with the downtrodden. She had rather a nice figure, too, if you liked your women tall and slender, which he definitely did not.

He indicated the tin pot. "If you would pour me a cup, I'll take some hair of the dog."

She knit her brow as she poured. "What does this mean?"

"A little nip, to clear my head in the mornings," he explained, and reached for his whiskey bottle. "How did your husband die?"

She shrugged as she watched him pour a tot of whiskey into the coffee. "I do not know. One morning, he is dead."

He took a sip of the fortified coffee and squinted at her. "How long ago?"

She considered this. "More than one year, but not two."

This corresponded with what he knew—so far, her story was checking out—and he said again, "My sympathies, Señora."

"*De nada*," she replied, without a trace of sorrow.

"Did you bury him up here?" He hadn't seen any evidence of a gravesite.

"I dragged him into a cave," she explained. "It was easier."

He nodded, a bit taken aback by the casual statement, but there was small blame to her, since it seemed apparent that she was on her own and it wouldn't be easy to dig a grave in this rocky soil. And it was true that there were a lot of caves, up along the crags; indeed, he'd hidden in one, back when he was monitoring Tosada. And it was a mighty stroke of luck, since it was in the cave that he'd first noted what seemed to be some promising indicators for gold.

Thus reminded that he'd best straighten-out this mess as soon as possible, he offered, "If you are agreeable, I will take you down the mountain—tomorrow, perhaps, because I should let my poor horse rest for a day. The mercantile agent in town took money from me that should rightfully be yours, if you're the one who owns this property."

This sparked her interest, and she raised her brows. "This is so?"

"Yes. We should both go to confront him."

She nodded her acquiescence, and then regarded him thoughtfully. "Why do you wish to live at this place?"

"I'm looking to raise some sheep, and to stay quiet for a couple of years." He added, "I come from Wales, and the Welsh know how to raise sheep."

This was the excuse he'd given the mercantile agent in town, and indeed, he planned to buy a few sheep to serve as a cover for his mining exploration. It was important that no one guess what his true purpose here was—gold tended to make men ruthless—and now there was the added problem of whether or not he truly owned the rights to mine the property. He'd have to be careful not to give the game away—not until he made sure everything was signed and sealed—and maybe not even then. His plan was to establish the mine and then go inform his former commander of the boon; the British army was sorely in need of funding, and it would be nothing short of a godsend to have access to a secret gold mine in the Spanish hills. All would be forgiven, and his commander would immediately restore him to the diplomatic service, so that he could take-up his former life again.

His companion continued to scrutinize him as she watched him drink his coffee, making no effort to mask her curiosity. "Why do you have no wife?"

He smiled slightly. "Why do you think I have no wife?"

"Do you?"

"No," he admitted. "I've been very busy for the past few years."

She nodded. "The war."

He nodded in return. "The war."

She cocked her head slightly. "You were a *guerrilla*? Is that how you know about this place? I know there were British soldiers who fought with the *guerrillas*."

"No," he said easily, hiding his alarm since the soldiers she referred to had been part of his own unit, and few knew of their existence. "I was an outfitter, and sold goods to the army."

Her brows rose. "*Si*? Then you must be rich."

He took another casual sip of his coffee, and duly noted that she was clever, and he should be a bit more careful about what he said to her. "I wish I was rich—it seems I am far too trusting."

In a sage manner, she nodded. "*Si*. You were cheated, with this land deal."

"Maybe—that remains to be seen. But if you indeed hold the title, once I get my money back from the agent, I will pay it to you instead and we can settle the matter between us. Do you have any kin in Spain, who will take you in?"

She seemed surprised by the question. "I will stay here; this is my home."

There was a small pause. "I don't know as we can both stay here," he explained diplomatically. The last needful thing was to have this woman underfoot—especially since he wasn't keen on anyone witnessing the sluice-box operation that he intended to set-up in the stream.

"You are the one who was tricked," she pointed out reasonably. "And I was here first."

He decided he wasn't going to argue, especially since he wasn't at all certain that she had indeed inherited this property from her husband; in general, he knew that Spanish inheritance laws weren't very kind to women. First things first, though; he'd find out if she was the owner, and if she was, then he'd have to think of an amenable solution to the problem —he could offer to give her a cut of the sheep-profits, and hope she'd be happy with that and leave him alone.

To this end, he offered a friendly smile. "I'll do a bit of hunting, this afternoon. The least I can do is bring-in some game for dinner."

"I have my chickens," she countered, unimpressed.

So; not the type to be softened-up. "Nevertheless, it will give me something to do."

She eyed his tin cup. "Can you shoot straight, after this hair from the dog?"

Holding on to his temper, he smiled again. "I suppose we shall see."

CHAPTER 3

The day after next, they began the journey down the mountain to the town of San Ysidro, Tremaine on his horse and Mora following behind him on her donkey. The descent was made in silence; she wasn't one to chatter—which was just as well, since he was rather wishing he could have managed another quick tot, to set him up for the day. But he'd been a bit stung by her remark about shooting straight, and so he was refraining, for the time being—which did nothing to help his frame of mind. The last needful thing was to have to listen to a chattering woman, and be forced to make polite conversation.

The previous day she'd left him to his own devices—again, much appreciated—asking only once if he needed something to eat. He'd responded by going out hunting along the foothills, and bringing back a brace of rabbits so as to give them to her—which did seem to be grudgingly appreciated, even though it was hard for him to read her.

He'd developed an instinct, when it came to assessing strangers—it was what had kept him alive, in his previous work—but he found that she was something of a puzzle. She seemed very self-contained—which was only to be expected, he supposed; she was from a different culture, and apparently had no qualms about living alone on a mountain and fending for herself. But she wasn't behaving as most women would in this situation, and it was unexpected, even as it was something of a relief.

As they neared the foot of the mountain, he advised, "Let me handle Señor Sanchez, if you would; I don't want to accuse him outright." This was his usual practice, from long experience; he always liked to come across as a friendly, naive Englishman—since there was no point in kicking up a battle and making the other person feel defensive, right off the mark. Better to engage in a civil manner, and find out as much as you could before deciding whether more forceful means would be necessary.

"*Si*," she agreed.

They came into San Ysidro, which was a bit larger than the other small villages that populated the region, thanks to its strategic location at the foot of the mountain. The town boasted a church, a bank, and a livery stable—along with an inn and a few other business establishments which were the direct result of its role in providing an alternate route for Napoleon's suppliers. Of course, the place had been busier during the war, and now it appeared to have sunk back into its former role as a sleepy little backwater town.

As they entered the town, Tremaine smiled and nodded in a friendly fashion to the banker, who was idly sitting on the porch in front of his establishment —best stay in the man's good graces; until he could get his feet beneath him, he may need a loan to get the mining operation off the ground.

They arrived at the mercantile agent's store, and after tying-up their animals, entered into the premises. The store was the main supplier of goods for the town, and its proprietor, Señor Sanchez, was a rather pompous little man who also acted as a general land agent; it was he who'd sold Tremaine his farming license.

Tremaine immediately noted that the shopkeeper's wary gaze rested on Mora, even though he greeted them with all appearance of cordiality. "Mademoiselle, Señor."

This seemed a bit odd—that Sanchez addressed Mora in such a way; she was a known widow, and she wasn't French. The man may have been misled about her heritage, though—perhaps Tosada had invented a French wife so as to obscure the fact she'd been the next thing to a slave. In any event, it didn't really matter—Tremaine had more pressing matters to attend to.

"*Buenos tardes,*" he greeted the other man amiably. "We have come because there seems to be some confusion; the Señora claims to own the homestead atop the mountain, and yet she is unaware that you drew-up a farming license for me."

The man frowned slightly, as his gaze rested upon Mora. "I believe the confusion is the Señora's; she does not own the property, it belonged to Señor Tosada and now it is owned by his brother, in Madrid."

Tremaine knit his brow. "But surely, as Tosada's widow wouldn't the Señora hold the rights to the property?"

After another wary glance at Mora, the man shook his head. "Not if Señora Tosada had no children with Señor Tosada. Under Spanish law, wives do not inherit if there are no children; instead, the land goes back to her husband's family." Almost kindly, he added, "You are not from Spain, and so you did not understand this, perhaps."

For the first time, Mora spoke. "No—it is you who does not understand, Señor. I did not inherit the land; instead, my husband deeded it to me. The deed is in the bank's vault, for safekeeping."

At this, both men stared at her in surprise. "This is true?" asked the agent.

"*Si.*" She paused, and then added, almost as an afterthought, "Do not cheat me, *kafir*."

"No, no," the man blustered; "It was a misunderstanding, only—"

"Easily verified," Tremaine offered, hiding his profound relief. "Let's go to the bank and clear this up."

The other man willingly came around the counter, and took his hat from the hook by the door. "I swear I did not know this, when I sold the license to you," he explained to Tremaine. "It is very unusual, for a man to do such a thing for his wife."

"Fair enough. Let's go check."

And so, the three walked across the dusty road to the bank, with Tremaine hiding his amusement because it seemed to him that the pompous agent was a bit intimidated by Tosada's foreign bride—his attitude had certainly taken a quick turnaround, after she'd spoken up.

The banker saw them approaching from his station on the porch, and rose to his feet; in contrast to the mercantile agent he was a slender man—older and more distinguished, as befit his calling.

Extending a hand to Tremaine, he asked affably. "I am Señor Ruiz; how may I help you, Señor?"

With a gesture toward the others, Tremaine explained, "There's been a bit of confusion over the rights to the homestead; Señora Tosada tells me that her husband deeded the property to her before he died."

"This is true," the man affirmed immediately. "The document sits in my vault."

"Ah—many thanks, this clears up our confusion. Is everything in order? You are certain?"

"Oh, yes; I applied the seal myself, señor." There was a slight pause, and then—weighing his words carefully—the banker added, "I believe Señor Tosada didn't want his creditors to know he owned the land—he was always a sly one, although I know I should not speak ill of the dead, *que el Señor le de descanso a su alma.*"

Tremaine turned to the mercantile agent. "Right; since that's been settled, I'd like my money back, please—it seems we were both operating under a false assumption."

"Of course, of course," Sanchez replied in an amiable manner that was a stark contrast to his earlier attitude. "Come back to my store, and I will give your refund."

Graciously, the banker offered, "If you would like to wait here in the shade, Señora, I will fetch lemon-water."

"*Gracias*," Mora replied, and settled into the chair that he'd just vacated.

The banker stood beside Mora's chair, as they both watched Tremaine step into the mercantile shop. In a low voice, he asked, "So; I should draw-up a deed, Mademoiselle?"

"Si," she replied, and took a sip of her lemon-water. "Make certain the date is from before."

"Bueno." He glanced at her from beneath his grizzled brows. "I have received a payment for you."

"Gracias," she replied, and accepted the small purse that he discreetly slipped into her hand, depositing it in her apron pocket.

"With respect, I have also been asked to convey a message to you."

"Say it, then."

"He says to be careful what you tell this man; he is shrewder than he seems."

Mora smiled slightly. "Si; I have learned this, already."

His duties discharged, the banker nodded. "When will the others be needed? Shall I arrange to send them up the mountain tomorrow, or is that too soon?"

"Day after tomorrow," she decided, her thoughtful gaze on the entry to the mercantile shop.

"Morning or evening?"

27

"Evening."

"Very good." He hesitated for a moment. "If I could send the dog today, Mademoiselle? He is not happy, and it makes me very uneasy."

She smiled again. "Si—you must not be made uneasy."

They then settled into silence, and awaited Tremaine's return.

CHAPTER 4

After Tremaine received his refund, he decided not to return up the mountain straightaway because there was no time like the present to purchase his sheep, now that he'd some money in hand. To this end, he left Mora to make a few purchases at the mercantile store and traveled to the end of town, where a rancher had a small holding.

He dismounted, and then rested his arms on the fence whilst he looked over the flock of sheep that grazed along the other side. As he did so, he thought over the meeting with the mercantile agent, and then the banker. Strange, that a Spaniard would deed his property over to a foreign bride, even if it was to escape his creditors. He must have trusted her, then

—even though by the looks of it he hadn't known her for very long. It was all very interesting, especially because he'd the uneasy feeling that it was all bit too pat—everything seemed a little too smooth, to him. Señor Sanchez was the sort of man to scorn an Englishman, and argue over the full refund—he knew the type—but the man had cooperated in undoing the deal as though butter wouldn't melt in his mouth. It didn't hit him right, for some reason. And by God, he could use a drink—he should have filled his hip flask this morning, so as to take the occasional nip with no one the wiser.

"You like my sheep, Señor?" The rancher approached along the fence on the opposite side, watching Tremaine with a speculative light in his eye. "You will buy?"

"*Si*—a half-dozen wethers, perhaps, just to see how they do on the mountain. If they do well, I will buy more."

The rancher nodded with approval as he gestured to the grazing sheep. "These will do well; they are good, hardy wethers."

"These are not wethers," Tremaine replied easily.

Feigning confusion, the man stammered, 'Oh—oh, of course, señor; my mistake."

With a nimble movement, Tremaine hoisted himself over the fence and walked over to a different group of sheep who were contained in a corral, cornering a few so that he could inspect them. He pried open their mouths, and then—with expert hands—pulled at their fleece with his fists, testing its thickness over various parts of the animal's body.

Watching him, the rancher had gone silent, and Tremaine glanced over at him. "What do you call these?"

"*Churras*, Señor."

"When's the fleece full?"

"Anytime in the autumn, Señor."

Tremaine nodded. "I'll take six, then. Along with a bottle of whiskey, if you have it."

"Of course, I have whiskey—I raise sheep," the man joked.

They bartered on the price, and after Tremaine counted out the coins, he walked over to his horse and took a long pull from the whiskey bottle before securing it in his saddlebag—ah, much better—he'd been a fool, not to have some close at hand; he shouldn't have let the woman nettle him.

And speaking of which, he could see that the nettlesome woman was approaching on her donkey. He was now feeling much less nettled, though, and so he teased, half-seriously, "Here's your last chance, if you'd like to stay in town."

"No," she declined with a touch of amusement. "You owe me money."

He laughed, and then searched along the bushes

on the side of the road for a likely switch. "I haven't forgot."

"I will not let you forget."

With all goodwill—Lord, he felt so much better—he said, "Come along, then. You can help me keep them from wandering off the trail."

The rancher opened the gate, and Tremaine mounted his horse, using the switch to steer the disorganized animals up the road. "Keep the leader moving in the right direction," he directed Mora. "Sheep tend to follow a leader."

"I know this; there were many sheep in my home country," she informed him. "They are very stupid, and I had not thought to tend them again."

He chuckled. "Well, you'll have to be reconciled, if you plan to stay at the homestead," he teased. "I'm sure these sheep aren't quite so stupid—they breed smarter sheep, here in Spain."

"If you say," she agreed with little enthusiasm.

"You'll make more money from the fleece, than from selling eggs," he pointed out. From what he could see, her only means of support seemed to be the chickens—presumably she was bartering eggs for necessities, which meant that she must be barely scratching by.

Which was one more problem to be piled atop the others—the last needful thing was to have this foreign woman underfoot, criticizing his habits and watching him set-up the mining operation. Try as he might, though, he could think of no workable solution; even if he had the means to set-up a separate house for her in town, she seemed bent on remaining at the homestead—and it was hers, after all. Unfortunately for him, her land was the key to his plan for redemption, and it was frustrating beyond measure that he didn't have the money to buy the land outright, and send her on her way.

They headed up the mountain trail—the going necessarily slow, as the sheep ambled along—and little was said for perhaps an hour. He then mentioned in a casual tone, "The winter will be harsh up there, so I may look to house the sheep in one of the caves along the foothills—it will keep them out of the wind. The barn's in a sorry state, and won't provide much shelter."

This was in keeping with the new plan he'd hatched; he'd herd the animals from the meadow to the caves, and—at least, for the time being—it would serve as a ready excuse to pursue his real purpose. He'd need to do a bit of exploring along the crags to decide if the site was worth the trouble, before he began any earnest work; there was gold nearly everywhere on earth, but it had to be present in sufficient quantities to make a mining enterprise worthwhile.

And then—if it did seem that the effort would be worth it—secrecy was even more important, in that he intended to turn the gold over to the British army. Plenty of Spaniards would take strong objection to this plan; Spain's army needed funding, too, and the gold—after all—was on Spanish land.

But that would be his old commander's concern; by that time, he'd have rejoined his old unit and be back in the thick of things, where he belonged. It was just as well—mining was a back-breaking business, and he'd left that kind of life far behind.

They continued their trek, with Tremaine using his switch to keep the sheep moving along. Mora—as was usual—said very little, and when they paused to let the animals rest for a minute, he offered, "I fully intend to pay you for the rights, but I'll be honest; I don't have much money, just now. If it is agreeable, I can pay some now, and then I will deliver the remainder after I start making money—shearing season will be in a couple of months."

He waited for her response even as he felt it a reasonable offer; after all, she hadn't been counting on the money to begin with, and so it would serve as an unlooked-for boon.

She smiled her half-smile; he was becoming familiar with this expression—as though she found everything slightly amusing. "I think you should marry me, instead," she said.

Astonished, he stared at her. *"What?"*

At his reaction, she lifted the corner of her mouth

in amusement. "I should have waited until you drank more of your whiskey, before speaking of this."

He drew his brows down, annoyed that he'd been caught-out. "You can't be serious—we barely know each other."

"It would be a good solution," she continued, as though it didn't much matter to her, one way or another. "You would own the land, and I would help you with your sheep."

Firmly, he replied. "No—although thank you for the offer."

She'd managed to get him nettled, again—he shouldn't have reacted so strongly, but it was beyond ridiculous to think that someone like him would marry someone like her. Although to be fair, she did make a good point; if he married her, there would be no question about the rights to the land—as her husband, they'd be his. As Señor Sanchez had pointed out, the Spanish property laws paid little heed to women.

She shrugged, and it was clear her feelings weren't hurt—she didn't seem to have feelings, in the first place. "I do not think you can do this alone."

"I appreciate the offer, Mora, but I intend to try."

"You should not drink, then."

Since this touched a nerve, he retorted, "That is

none of your business, and I will thank you not to mention it again."

She was silent for a few minutes, as their animals resumed their walk alongside the ambling sheep, and he was trying to decide if he owed her an apology for being so sharp when she observed, "If the raiders come, you will need someone who is sober enough to shoot at them."

Suddenly alert, he turned to gaze at her. "What raiders are these?"

She shrugged. "They come at night, to take their loot through the pass. I shoot at them, so they do not come too close."

This was of interest, but on second thought, not much of a surprise. Since the *Afrancesados* had used the place as a way-station to smuggle supplies to Napoleon, there was every possibility that the raiders she spoke of were left-over *Afrancesados* from that operation, putting their knowledge of the secret route to good use. "Thanks for the warning."

"*Si*—we must not let them steal your precious sheep." She was teasing him again, in her semi-grave manner.

"Now I know how you came to be so handy with a weapon," he teased in return, rather relieved that they were on a good footing again. "You've had plenty of practice."

"*Si*," she agreed. "Plenty of practice."

The sheep suddenly paused and raised their heads, startled, and Tremaine looked about him with his hand on his pistol; usually such behavior signified that a predator was nearby.

To his surprise, however, he sighted a large dog, trotting up the mountain after them.

CHAPTER 5

The dog was an unusual breed for these parts—thin and sleek, with long legs and a long, curling tail. He was tan-colored with short, coarse hair and didn't look to be aggressive, as he approached them with his tongue lolling out, and his short ears laid back.

Nevertheless, Tremaine eyed him warily as his hand continued to rest on his pistol. He didn't want to risk losing a sheep, but the dog didn't seem intent on attack—didn't appear to be feral—but instead he seemed well-fed and healthy. Tremaine was loath to shoot him, being as he'd fond memories of the sheepdog they'd had when he was growing up—one of the only fond memories he had from his childhood. "Go home," he shouted, and made a menacing gesture. "Go home."

In response, the dog immediately sat down at a small distance.

"He is well-behaved," Mora noted.

"I am more worried that he is hungry," Tremaine explained.

"He does not seem so—he may be lost."

"Let's keep moving," Tremaine decided as he took up his reins. To the dog, he firmly commanded "Stay," and held up a hand in a gesture the shepherds back home used. The commands might be universal—although this didn't look to be a herding dog—he looked more like those racing dogs that were bred for sport, save that he was a bit bulkier, and his head was wider.

They began moving again, and Tremaine glanced over his shoulder to see that the dog was again following them, keeping his distance.

"He'll find his way home again," Tremaine suggested. "Just ignore him."

But as it turned out, the dog followed them all the way up to the homestead, and then sat placidly—again, at a distance—whilst Tremaine paused to allow the sheep to drink from the stream, and graze in the open meadow.

"Don't feed him," Tremaine warned Mora. "He needs to go back home."

"*Si*," she agreed.

He then gestured toward the sheep. "If you'll

watch over them, I'll make sure the barn is secure, before I turn them in for the night."

"*Si,*" she agreed again.

He went into the barn to make certain there were no gaps or weaknesses from which the animals could escape, and then he rubbed-down his tired horse. Pausing to take a drink before he went outside again, he decided that it was a day well-spent, all in all. If Mora was thinking that perhaps he'd be willing to marry her—small chance, of course—it meant that she wouldn't interfere with his farming rights in the hope that he might change his mind. And—honestly—she couldn't be blamed her for broaching the subject; he was British, and the British held the whip-hand on the Continent at the present time. She was from a part of the world where marriages were arrangements, and so she'd seized on this opportunity to secure her future—no doubt she'd like the protection of having a husband again, and a British one, at that. Not to mention she could use a man's help, if she truly intended to live here at the homestead.

Idly, he took another pull from the bottle as he thought about it. She was a bit of an enigma; he continued to have the sense that there was more to her than met the eye, but she seemed amiable enough—and if she meant him any harm, she'd already had more than enough opportunity. More likely she was someone—like himself—who was trying to find a path forward, after life had abruptly taken an unwelcome turn.

Speaking of such, he decided with some reluctance to put the bottle down and get on with planning-out his mining operation. He'd the sheep, now, and events were in train—there was no putting it off. First thing tomorrow morning, he'd go explore the caves along the crags, and see what there was to see.

When he walked out of the barn to gather-up the sheep for the night, he noted with some surprise that Mora was sitting on her haunches, and playing with the dog.

"Mora," he warned. "He needs to go home."

"Watch," she replied, and tossed a stick, which the dog raced to recover and bring back, clearly delighted that she was engaging with him.

"I think he's been well-trained," Tremaine acknowledged. "But that only means that someone must be missing him."

"I suppose," she agreed, and rose to her feet. "Shall I make coffee?"

"No, thanks," he replied easily, hiding his annoyance that she was hinting he was drunk, again. "I'm going to turn-in early. Tomorrow morning, I'll go scout-out the caves, to find the best one for housing the sheep; don't be surprised if I'm gone by the time you're up."

"Good night, then," she said, and turned to walk into the house.

Tremaine watched her go, a bit surprised because he'd half-expected an attempt at seduction, now that she'd mentioned a possible marriage between them. And there'd be plenty of incentive; he was a gentleman, and she might hope that a pregnancy would force his hand. But she didn't seem the least interested in bed-sport—wasn't behaving like most women would in this situation—which was a bit refreshing, truth to tell. In his line of business, he'd often had to deal with seductive women who had ulterior motives.

As he walked around to gather-up the sheep, he was somewhat surprised to feel a twinge of disappointment that she hadn't even bothered to make the attempt.

CHAPTER 6

The next morning, Tremaine started out toward the caves a bit later than he would have liked, being as he'd been unable to resist a dram or two the night before and was now suffering for it. Not that he could be blamed, of course; he was sleeping in a hay-crib amongst a herd of sheep and a flock of chickens—it was a miracle he got any sleep at all. Nothing for it; he'd have to negotiate with Mora to sleep in the house—maybe on the floor by the hearth. But he'd best keep his wits about him; human nature was human nature, and they were both young and healthy. Not to mention that she was attractive, in her own way—not to his taste, of course, but a lot of men liked that type; slim, exotic women.

As he mounted his horse—poor fellow wasn't getting much rest, for someone his age—he realized he should have asked Mora to let the sheep out to graze while he was away. But no doubt she'd figure it out on her own—she seemed very practical. And he didn't see any sign of the dog, which was to the good—the rascal must have decided to finally go home. Interesting, that he'd decided to follow them up the mountain—maybe he'd lived here, once upon a time.

He rode across the meadow to the outcropping of rock he'd once lurked behind—back when he was monitoring who and what was going through the pass—and found that little had changed. After hobbling his horse, he climbed up the rocky terrain, his gaze intent on the stone beneath his feet as he looked for placer minerals—tell-tale signs that gold was nearby.

He came to the cave where he'd slept for a few days—and bent his head to walk within. It had been a useful vantage point, the last time he was here; the entry was hidden from casual view behind another outcropping, and there were several other caves further up the rock walls that would allow for a quick retreat, if it had been necessary.

If he was honest with himself, he'd admit that one of the reasons he was eager to come back to this place was because he'd rather enjoyed lurking in the cave —it reminded him of home; or at least, of the fonder memories he had of home—back when he was optimistic about a future far away from Wales. But there was nothing like conducting espionage during a long and bloody war to make a person's world-view change, and now he felt an almost nostalgic fondness for his eager, younger self. Perhaps he'd find that person again, if only things would go his way—for once—and he could get this dubious prospect to pay off. It was the only thing that had kept him going, through those first dark days—the thought of making things right again, and rejoining his comrades. If only he hadn't let everyone down—

Drawing a deep breath, he shook his head to clear it. He had to stop dwelling on it; instead, he should think about how satisfying it was going to be to redeem himself, and show everyone he could be counted on, yet again.

The recesses of the cave were dark, and so he paused to light a lantern. Then—with his hand trailing on the rocky wall—he followed the narrow passageway until he came to a small, cleared-out area that lay within the recesses of the cave. The area was perhaps ten feet wide, and he noted again what had caught his interest the first time he'd come across it; there was a patch of sunlight, reflected on the floor.

Indeed, if you craned your head, you could see a glimpse of the sky though an opening overhead, at the peak where the cave's walls joined together. A casual explorer might assume that this ceiling-opening had been carved-out so as to allow a campfire in these close quarters, but if you were a miner, your mind leapt immediately to another interpretation.

With a great deal of satisfaction, he crouched and observed what he'd noticed last time; the tell-tale cracks and blackening along the wall where someone had conducted huffing operations—an ancient mining method that used fire to extract gold from rock.

With a growing sense of excitement, he explored the crevices in the blackened wall with his fingertips. There was gold within; he could *feel* it—and if there was gold in this rock face, there would be gold in the stream that ran through these crags and continued on through the meadow—it was miles easier to extract gold from a river than by lighting stone with fire. Would the vein be rich enough to make a mining operation worthwhile? He'd find out—he need only purchase some lumber, build a rudimentary sluice-box in the stream, and then see what panned out. Lord, but it had been a long time since he'd felt this encouraged; finally, finally, something was going to go his way.

Rising, he held the lantern before him as he ventured a bit further along the narrow passageway —he didn't remember seeing any other indications of huffing, but he hadn't had time to fully explore the depths of the caves because he was supposed to be monitoring the homestead, and couldn't leave his post for long.

It seemed, however, that whoever had carved-out that overhead vent hadn't created any others along the ceiling, which was a problem if he looked to conduct a little huffing operation, himself. It was dangerous to light a fire in a cave; even with a vent, the fumes could be deadly. Of course, if he thought it worthwhile, he could always hire a few men to carve-out another vent or two; it would all depend on whether the vein that ran along this wall was rich enough to start an operation.

He halted suddenly, as his gaze rested upon a huddled object lying against the wall, about a dozen feet further ahead. He listened, but heard only silence—he was certain there was no other person in the cave, even though the object looked to be a bedroll of some sort—someone must have left it behind. As he came closer, however, the lantern-light revealed what appeared to be a cadaver, sewn into a makeshift shroud.

Crouching, he reviewed it dispassionately. Tosada, presumably; Mora had said she'd pulled him into a cave rather than bury him, which only made sense—especially if he died in winter, when the ground would be rock-solid. Any of these caves would make a fitting sepulcher, and she didn't seem the sentimental type, who'd want to tend her husband's grave.

Pulling his knife, he cut a few threads so as to take a look. The body had decomposed—but it seemed clear he'd been a middle-aged Spanish man, as could be expected. What wasn't to be expected, however, was the fact there was a hole from a musket-ball, plainly visible on the dead man's breast bone.

CHAPTER 7

When Tremaine returned to the homestead, he staggered a bit when he dismounted from the horse—he'd drank a little too much from his flask on the ride home and small blame to him, considering his alarming find. Best to wash up in the stream before going in to confront Mora—he'd need his wits about him.

After splashing the cold water on his face, he felt a bit less fuzzy and ducked through the entry door, where a delicious smell met his senses. Rabbit stew, it seemed; she'd a kettle on an iron stand over the hearth, and was chopping various vegetables on the wooden table before tossing them into the kettle with an expert flick of her fingers.

He suddenly realized that he was hungry—he'd forgot to eat, today—but first things first. Without preamble, he began, "I took a look into the caves across the meadow. It seems your husband took a musket-ball."

She didn't even look up, as she continued to chop a turnip. "That is not my husband."

He raised his brows and carefully settled onto a stool. "Oh? Who is he?"

"An outlaw. He tried to steal my chickens."

He stared at her graceful, nimble fingers for a moment, processing this. "So, you shot him."

"*Si*," she affirmed, and glanced over at him with a hint of amusement.

Frowning slightly, he ventured, "You know, Mora, I am beginning to think you are something of an outlaw, yourself."

She smiled her grave smile, as though pleased by this characterization. "If you say."

He cocked his head, amused despite himself. "Should I be worried? How many men have you killed?"

"Too many to count," she replied, as she continued to chop.

"I bet I've killed more," he teased.

She glanced over at him for a moment. "No, you are not hard, like me. You feel things too much; this is how we are different."

A bit affronted, he insisted, "I'm hard when I need to be."

She gathered the remaining vegetables between her hands—sweeping them up from the table—and after she turned to toss them into the kettle, she said, "My father sold me to a terrible man, who beat me, and did terrible things. So, I killed him, and then I killed my father, too, so that my sisters would be free. We were smuggled out of Algiers on a ship—we had to walk through tunnels, underground."

Tremaine stared at her for a moment, bereft of speech. "Good Lord."

She nodded. "We landed at a convent in France, and I was told that if I wished, I could be a Christian nun." She paused, and flicked him a sidelong glance. "I said no."

He chuckled, and she smiled. "So, they found me a husband who needed a strong wife."

He blew out a breath. "That's an extraordinary story."

Nodding, she bent over the kettle to stir the contents; pushing back a tendril of hair that had escaped from her head-scarf.

He watched her in the flickering firelight and suddenly thought—Lord; I think I like her, a little. Can't let myself get involved, though; she's more along the lines of a camp-follower—rough around the edges, and a bit too savvy for my taste. I like my girls shy and sweet.

Thinking of this, he observed, "You'd be just the

type of girl my commander would recruit to be a spy, if there was still a war going. He tended to look for orphans who'd already shown a ruthless streak."

She smiled indulgently as she stirred the stew. "Oh? Who was your commander?"

Suddenly aware that he was contradicting the story he'd told her before—he'd drunk too much, and let this be a lesson—he offered vaguely, "An old sergeant-major, who came to a sad end at Vitoria."

Thinking to change the subject—Lord, he'd slipped up—he asked, "How much ammo do you have? If we have to deal with raiders on a regular basis, we may need more."

"I use shot, in my musket," she explained, and indicated the heaps of small pebbles that were lining the hearth. "There are many of these pebbles in the stream—many, many. They make for good shot."

He watched her for a moment. "The dead fellow was killed with a musket-ball, though."

"I shot him with his own pistol," she explained, as she set out two tin plates, along with a small loaf of fresh-baked bread.

"Nice work. Where's the pistol?"

"It is in my holster," she explained, as though speaking to a child.

"But yours is an English pistol." He'd wondered at this, when he'd first seen it—wondered how she'd got hold of a fine English pistol.

She glanced over at him in amusement. "The dead man had an English pistol. You do not trust me, I think."

Slowly, he admitted, "I'm wondering—I'm wondering how many others there are, in the caves."

She began to spoon out the stew onto the plates. "I told you, I have killed many men. I think you do not listen."

Bluntly, he asked, "Did you kill your husband?"

"No," she replied evenly.

He stared down at his stew for a moment, wishing his mind felt a bit sharper. "I think—I think there are things you're not telling me." He paused, wishing he hadn't said it aloud—Lord, he was botching this, but it was hard to think clearly.

"*Si*," she agreed, as she took her seat opposite him. "There are many things I am not telling you."

He decided to pass it off as a joke, and spread his hands. "Then how do I know you are not going to kill me, too?"

"I like you." Thoughtfully, she took a bite of her stew. "I think I will marry you."

"Oh—as for that," he dissembled, "I'm afraid I am already promised."

She made a sound of disappointment, before taking another spoonful of stew. "That is very much a shame; what is her name?"

"Lisabetta," he replied, saying the first name that came into his rather befuddled head.

"Lisabetta is lucky. I will tease you no more." With an efficient movement, she scooped a few spoonfuls of her stew into a tin cup, and then went to the door to whistle. To Tremaine's surprise, the dog trotted up to the stoop, and she bent to give him the cup.

"He's still here?" he asked in surprise.

"*Si*," she agreed. "Still here."

CHAPTER 8

Tremaine was back in the caves the next day to do more exploring, mainly because he'd decided he needed to separate from Mora for a time, and gather-up his wits. He'd been a fool to confront her about the dead man, so late in the day like that—he tended to be a bit less focused, late in the day—and now he was trying to decide if there was something rather ominous about all this.

During the war, he'd become adept at subterfuge —at portraying different identities, depending on whatever infiltration was needed—and he'd the feeling—he'd the uncomfortable feeling that the roles were reversed, this time, and it was he who was being infiltrated; that she was outwitting him, in some way.

Of course, he was out of practice—his

commander hadn't put him on an infiltration assignment in years; instead he'd been working behind-the-scenes more and more—but still and all, he couldn't shake the feeling that there was an undercurrent here; something perhaps even dangerous.

But if that were the case, it was unclear what her aim would be; he'd no money and no prospects—save for this farming interest, which would mean nothing to her since she owned the land outright. That it was somehow connected to his work during the war was a possibility—it seemed almost too much a coincidence, otherwise—but for the life of him, he couldn't understand why he'd attracted anyone's attention at all. He was no longer working for the service, and—truth to tell—he hadn't been trusted with any secret information in a donkey's age. And—after all—he hadn't been led here; he'd come on his own, and it hadn't been an easy thing, actually. It all made little sense.

With no small relief, he decided that he was imagining things—imagining that Mora had some ulterior purpose. She may not have been honest with him—even though every word of her story rang true—but to be fair, he'd not been honest with her, either, and it was not unexpected; they'd both sustained some hard knocks in life, and it seemed that neither one of them had any supporters at the present time—at least they did have that in common. Which was no doubt why she was hinting at marriage; as a single woman she was vulnerable, and a British husband would give her a measure of security. His imagination was working overtime—to think she had the upper hand, somehow, and that he was just a means to an end. He'd nothing to offer, and he was just being fanciful.

Hard on this thought, he heard a small sound behind him, and whirled to draw his pistol only to see the dog, regarding him steadily as he wagged his curling tail.

"Hallo, fellow," he said, and crouched to hold out a hand.

But the dog wheeled and darted out of the cave—he was a sleek, muscular animal who could move like quicksilver; a hunting breed, no doubt—just not one you saw much around these parts. He seemed a bit people-shy—although he was willing to trust Mora, apparently, which stood as a good sign; dogs were good indicators, when it came to people.

Reminded, he debated whether to return to the homestead for a mid-day meal—maybe she'd made more stew, or had even roasted a chicken. The stew last night had been very welcome—there were days when he'd forget to eat, and yesterday had been one of them.

He emerged from the cave, and almost immediately fell down to flatten himself against the rock; he could hear raucous laughter, caught in the wind that was drifting up the mountain. Men's voices—and they were coming from the homestead.

The raiders, he thought in acute alarm; and it definitely didn't sound as though Mora had chased them off, this time—he was certain he'd have heard gunfire. Had they captured her?

Straining his ears, he listened, and tried to gauge the situation—he didn't hear a woman's voice, frightened or otherwise, and the men seemed to be inactive—it sounded as though they were joking about and taking their leisure, after the hard ride up the mountain.

Carefully, he crept out on a rocky outcropping so as to peer over its edge. He couldn't see the men—they were inside the building—and the meadow was empty; a shame that he couldn't see if Mora's donkey remained in the barn, or if she'd managed to flee. Was she hiding, somewhere? There would be no hiding in the open meadow, and he'd be an easy target, himself, if he tried to ride across it to the homestead.

Instead, he'd create a diversion and flush them out so as to start picking them off. His musket was on his horse—lucky he'd brought it with him—and even though he was out-of-range for an accurate shot, he could at least try to scare them off. He would start shooting, and hope they weren't in the mood for a firefight.

Pressed against the rock, he'd begun to sidle sideways in the direction of his horse when he suddenly heard his name whispered.

"Tremaine."

With an enormous sense of relief, he jerked his head around and beheld Mora, lying flat on a rocky crag just above him. "Lord, Mora; you made me jump," he whispered. "Are you all right?"

"*Si*," she replied. Nimbly, she scrambled down the rocks to lay beside him, as they watched the activity at the homestead.

"It sounds as though they have found your whiskey," she noted.

With immense frustration, he observed, "Yes. And those bastards are going to steal my sheep."

But she disagreed. "I do not think so—they will not wish to herd sheep over the pass."

He nodded, since that made sense. "Right. But if they're leaving over the pass, they may see our animals when they come this way—and my musket's on my horse."

"Should we go fetch it, and try to rout them out?" she asked, as though this would be an ordinary task. "If we shoot at them, they may leave without taking anything."

"No—we'd best stay hidden," he replied rather firmly. "We're outnumbered, and I won't chance it. And even if they see the animals, I doubt they'll come hunting for us up here, since we've the higher ground, and they'd be exposed."

"*Si*," she agreed, rather reluctantly. "Then I will show you a good hiding-place." She made a gesture, indicating the wall of rock above them.

"Right," he agreed. "Let's go."

CHAPTER 9

Mora had led him to an almost invisible crevice in the rock face, that—when you sidled through, sideways—led into a small cave. They'd been hiding-out for perhaps an hour, leaning against the rocky entry so as to watch the activity in the meadow below—not a lot going on, just now, but snatches of men's voices could be heard when the wind was headed in the right direction.

Straining to listen, Tremaine decided that he wasn't familiar with whatever dialect the raiders were speaking—he couldn't make out the words themselves, but the cadence didn't sound Spanish. Which meant they weren't *Afrancesados*, so that belied his earlier theory that any raiders would be leftover *Afrancesados* from Tosada's operation.

It also meant they weren't Spanish *guerrillas*—unless, perhaps they spoke a language that didn't sound Spanish. But the raiders' behavior made this unlikely in the first place; *guerrillas* excelled in stealth and undercover work—it was the reason they'd wreaked such havoc during the war—and they wouldn't be quite so brazen. But whoever they were, it was to be devoutly hoped that they would depart with all speed; he would soon be in a bad way.

"It's cold in here," he offered, mainly to excuse the fact that his hands were starting to tremble. He crossed his arms so as to bury them in his armpits—Lord, he needed a drink.

Nonetheless, he needed to keep his wits about him so as to strategize, and to this end he said to her, "I doubt they will try to come up here, even if they see our animals—they'd be at a huge disadvantage. But if they are drunk enough to try, I need you to obey orders; I will start shooting so to give you cover to escape over the top."

She considered this for a moment, and then pointed out, "You would have the better chance to escape over the top, Tremaine. Perhaps I should give you cover, and you can circle back over the peak, to attack them from behind."

"I'm not going to leave you here to face them alone," he said firmly. "I'll have your promise, here and now."

"*Si*; I promise," she agreed.

After perhaps another hour, Tremaine decided that he'd best sit down, to obscure the trembling in his legs. He settled-in next to the dog, who was lying beside Mora as she kept watch.

"When it is full dark, we will light a fire," Mora offered.

"It's too dangerous, to light a fire in here," he explained, and then paused for a moment because his voice sounded querulous to his own ears. More calmly, he continued, "There is no vent in the ceiling, to allow the smoke to escape."

She glanced back at him. "There is a vent. It is further back in the cave."

"Is that so?" he asked, suddenly alert. "I'll go have a look."

Because his legs were a bit unsteady, he braced his hands against the rock wall and sidled through the narrow confines until he came to a hewn-out area, similar to the one he'd seen in the lower cave. With a great deal of satisfaction, he observed another blackened wall with a vent overhead; another ancient huffing operation—and another confirmation that someone else had seen what he'd seen—the tell-tale signs that there was gold in this mountain.

He crouched, trying to gather himself, and wished he didn't feel this almost overwhelming sense of dread; thus far, the raiders had shown no signs of leaving the homestead, and if he was forced to spend the night here, things could get a bit dicey. Hard on this thought, his hands started trembling again, and he tucked them under his arms again.

"I will light a fire," Mora said, from behind him.

"Lord, you can creep up on a man," he said irritably. It was true; she could move very silently—it was a bit unnerving.

She didn't respond, but stacked the dried wood that was at hand within the stone-circle that had been already built on the dirt floor. She then produced a strike-box and carefully lighted the kindling, blowing on the embers until the flames emerged.

She'd obviously done this many times before, and so he asked, "Was this your favorite bolt-hole?"

She smiled her grave smile. "What does this mean?"

"A place to hide."

"*Si*," she agreed. "My favorite bolt-hole."

"I may have to go outside for a bit," he said abruptly. "I'm not feeling well."

Her thoughtful gaze rested on him for a moment. "Oh? If you will lie down, I will make a broth for you."

He blinked, unhappy that she'd stymied his excuse to get away from her; he'd gone through what was coming a couple of times before, and it wasn't something he'd want another person to witness. "Right—well, I'll go outside, just for a moment." He'd been a fool not to bring an extra flask, but on the other hand he'd no idea that he'd be stuck here, in a cave with her. It was a damnable situation, and would not be getting better any time soon.

"Lie down," she said in a firm tone. "Lie down, Tremaine—here is a blanket."

"It is cold," he agreed, as he wrapped the blanket around him. He then began to shake uncontrollably, and decided he could hide it better if he did lie down. Miserably, he clenched his teeth and cursed himself for landing in this situation.

He lay silently, battling his body and paying little attention to her until she suddenly pressed a cup to his mouth. "Here, drink," she said.

"No—no," he protested, suddenly wary.

Relentlessly, she pressed the cup against his clenched teeth. "You must drink, Tremaine. It will help."

In the face of her insistence, he managed to drink a swallow. It wasn't warm, whatever it was, and it tasted bitter—definitely not a broth. "Dreadful," he managed, his teeth chattering.

"A little more," she coaxed.

"No—leave me alone, Mora."

She waited, with her cup poised, and then he realized that the shaking was subsiding, and that a slow warmth was spreading through his bones.

"You see?" she asked.

"Right," he mumbled, and managed to drink the remainder.

"Lie down, now, and sleep," he heard her say—but she seemed far away, and her voice seemed to echo oddly.

"No—" He tried to open his eyes, but discovered that his eyelids were too heavy, and would not obey command. Keenly aware that he was not acquitting himself very well, he managed to say, "We will take turns, keeping watch."

"Of course," she soothed, and laid a reassuring hand on his forehead.

It was the first time she'd touched him, and he suddenly wondered if seduction was indeed her aim—not that he could manage it; Lord, he couldn't even open his eyes. Cautiously he murmured, "You're very attractive; don't think I'm not tempted. I'm a gentleman, though."

"Good," she said, a thread of amusement in her voice. "Go to sleep, now."

"The dog—" Agitated, he fought to stay awake because there was something about the dog—something that wasn't right—

"The dog will keep watch, too," she teased.

He tried to smile, but found that he couldn't seem to control the muscles in his face. And it was so pleasant, to lie here, warm and relaxed. So very, very, pleasant.

CHAPTER 10

On the third or fourth attempt, Tremaine managed to open his eyes and found that he was staring at the rocky cave ceiling; it was daylight, but he'd the sense that a lot of time had passed. Blinking, he slowly managed to gather-up his wits—the raiders, and Mora. What had happened?

Listening, he heard only silence, and then he turned his head to the side and saw that she was not in the cave with him. Instead, the dog was seated at a small distance, watching him and wagging his tail, upon meeting his gaze.

Tremaine licked his lips—his mouth was as dry as cotton-wool. "Where's Mora?" he managed, and the dog immediately wheeled and trotted out the passageway.

Gingerly, he propped himself up on an elbow, and

stretched his neck, which was stiff—he'd lain a long time, on the hard floor. Days, perhaps?

The dog trotted into the cleared area, with Mora close behind. "I have water," she said, and handed him a flask.

He lifted it to his lips and drank it dry, somewhat bemused that Mora—true to form—wasn't volunteering any information. "The raiders?"

"They are gone." She made an impatient sound. "They took the horse and the donkey."

He drew a deep breath, and considered this bad news. "They took my musket, then."

"I have other muskets."

He eyed her, since he'd taken a careful inventory of the weapons in the homestead, out of habit. "I don't remember seeing any muskets."

"They are hidden," she explained.

"Good. We'll have to walk down to the town, and buy some more horses."

"When you are stronger," she said firmly. "You must eat, and rest."

The air was heavy with the unspoken reason for his weakness, and he decided he was being childish not to speak of it—especially since she'd nursed him through. With a sense of stoic resolution, he offered, "Thank you for taking care of me, Mora. I was in a bad way."

"You will have no more whiskey," she advised

bluntly. "You must promise, because you are a gentleman."

He stared at her, equal parts surprised and embarrassed. "It's a trifling thing, Mora. I've gone without before—I can give it up whenever I want."

"It is bad for you," she replied in all seriousness. "And so, you must have no more. In my country it is forbidden, and this is how it must be for you."

Thoroughly annoyed, he retorted, "It's none of your business."

"It is all my business," she replied in an even tone. "I am going to help you dig your gold, but I will not live with a drunkard."

He stared at her in abject dismay, and then quickly controlled his reaction. "What gold? What are you talking about?"

"When you were not in your right mind, you spoke of the gold in the walls." She paused and lifted her gaze to the cave walls. "It was very surprising."

He drew a hand over his face, taking the moment to try to marshal his thoughts. "I was clean out of my mind," he said firmly. "I must have been dreaming."

"You do not trust me," she acknowledged with a small shrug. "I do not blame you. But you will need help, I think."

There was a small silence, whilst he thought through how he should respond; it was her land, after all, and if she was determined to stay here, she'd soon see what he was about. That, and there was the obvious fact that if she wanted to dispose of him and seize his claim, she'd already had the perfect opportunity—he'd been as helpless as a kitten.

Weighing what to say, he decided to admit, "I think there may be gold in this mountain, and I think someone tried to mine it at some point—maybe even as far back as the Romans. I'd like to buy some lumber and make a sluice-box, to see if a mining operation would be worthwhile."

She narrowed her eyes, listening intently. "What is this sloo-box?"

"It's a wooden box that makes it easier to mine gold from a stream—miles easier than panning by hand."

Knitting her brow in confusion, she asked, "Is the gold in the water, or in the walls?"

"Both, with any luck." Reminded, he assured her, "Since it is your land, I will give you a portion of whatever I find."

She made an impatient sound. "No—do not be a fool. We must marry."

He raised his brows in surprise. "We must?"

In practical manner, she pointed out, "If there is gold, it must be clear who owns the land."

Diplomatically, he explained, "I do appreciate the offer, Mora, but I won't be staying here very long, even if I strike gold. I think another war will break out soon, and I'll want to go help in the fight."

She thought about this, for a moment. "Isn't it more important that you stay here, and dig your gold?"

He stared at her, because suddenly he realized that he hadn't thought any further than redeeming himself in the eyes of his former colleagues, and taking back his old life again. But she made a good point; if he did strike gold, it was far more important that he secure its secret delivery to British forces— and no sacrifice would be too great to achieve this end. He'd been so intent upon making things right in his personal affairs that he hadn't thought it through —that funding Wellington's army would be miles more important than taking-up his former life again. And he'd need help with this prospect—at least until he could contact his old commander, and lay the plan before him.

"We should get married," he abruptly agreed.

She nodded as though this was a foregone conclusion. "And then, whether you stay or go, I will stay."

He couldn't help but smile. "You like living here." He'd already come to this conclusion; it must seem worlds away from the desert where she'd grown up.

Thoughtfully, she nodded. "*Si.* It is very different, to live here. It makes me very different."

"I'm the opposite; this area is similar to my home, back in Wales."

She eyed him speculatively. "But you did not like it, there. You never speak of it."

"I did not like the people who were there," he corrected. With a hand braced against the stone wall, he managed to rise to his feet, and decided, after a moment, that he was fit to walk. "Let's get back to the homestead; I'm starving."

CHAPTER 11

They walked across the meadow to the homestead, Tremaine using a branch as a walking-staff because he was still a bit weak. He'd gone through this before, on those occasions when he'd tried to swear-off the whiskey, and it was always a terrifying few days. Whatever Mora had given him had knocked him out during the worst of it, and now he was a little weak—mainly because he hadn't eaten.

At least his mind was feeling clearer, and he was reminded that he'd missed something rather obvious; the fact that the supposed stray dog was constantly watching Mora's face, as though awaiting a command. It seemed obvious that he was her dog, but for some reason she'd pretended that he wasn't. This subterfuge made little sense, and he continued to have the feeling—stronger, now—that she wasn't at all what she seemed. It didn't not bode well—especially now that she knew about the gold—but if this was some sort of trap, she'd had plenty of time to spring it—he'd been completely helpless.

And in the end, he'd little choice but to trust her, since first, she owned the land, second, he'd told her about the gold and third, apparently this near-stranger was going to be his wife.

The fact that he wasn't rebelling strongly against such an idea just went to show how his priorities had changed—in a strange way, he'd matured, there in the cave, and was thinking beyond himself, for once. Marriage would secure the land, and—if there was gold to be had—it would be a necessary sacrifice for the British cause. Not to mention that he was a gentleman, and he should protect Mora—she'd helped him through a rough time, and he was grateful. Perhaps they would rub along together reasonably well; she was not at all like any other woman he'd known, and it was rather refreshing, in an odd way.

As they neared the homestead, he could hear the chickens squawking in annoyance. "The chickens are starving, too," he observed.

"*Si*," she agreed. "I will feed them. I will collect some eggs, and make a *paella*."

"Much appreciated. I'll go wash in the stream—I'm a bit ripe."

She headed toward the barn as he turned to the stream, stripping off his shirt and suddenly struck by the odd fact that the raiders hadn't stolen the chickens. He'd stolen a chicken or two himself, when he's been traversing the countryside, and there was nothing like knowing you have fresh meat tied to your saddlebags for those times when you could pause to light a fire.

Gingerly, he lowered himself into the coldness of the stream and lay in the shallows, letting the water run over him. He ducked his head under, and could hear the amplified rumbling of the running water as he contemplated his current situation. So; there was something very strange about all this, but for the life of him he couldn't fathom what it meant. The raiders had stolen his old horse—hardly worth the trouble—but had not helped themselves to the chickens that were there for the taking. And meanwhile, his wife-to-be had lied to him about her dog and—lest we forget—there was an unknown number of dead men, hidden away in the caves. Not to mention she'd a stockpile of weapons hidden away somewhere, too.

He raised his head from the stream, and then sat up, smoothing back his wet hair and considering these rather ominous facts. Idly flipping the water with a hand, he decided to was best to concentrate on what was known, rather than trying to puzzle-out the unknowns. The main take-away was that she didn't seem bent on killing him—since she'd plenty of chances—and he could swear she was sincere about wanting to help him mine the gold. If nothing else, her willingness to marry him seemed to prove it—it was a generous gesture, considering that she owned the land outright.

Although she would also want the protection that a British husband could afford her, which in turn reminded him that he'd indeed have an obligation to protect her, if she was to be his wife. To this end, he should travel to Gibraltar as soon as possible—the British garrison there would know how to get in touch with his old commander, since the man's operatives would be keeping a careful eye on the Mediterranean.

Originally, he'd planned to first make certain this dubious prospect was going to pay off before he approached his old spymaster in a cloud of glory, but now things had changed, and that fantasy seemed a bit childish. He'd have to take a more practical approach—he'd seen firsthand that Mora would be at risk, alone in this remote place. Therefore, he would contact his old commander immediately, explain his plan, and ask that a few men to be assigned as protection whilst he determined the merits of the mining operation.

He'd have to be discreet about conveying the message, of course; it went without saying that the gold would have to be secretly funneled to the British, if Spain was about to be caught-up in another war with Napoleon—after all, Spain had wound-up in enemy hands, last time around. Not to mention the *guerrillas* who'd fought to defend their country would want the gold to support their own efforts, and no one would blame them. But the British were the only ones capable of beating Napoleon again, and so to Wellington's army it would go—he didn't have any qualms about it, at all.

Idly, he scooped up some of the pebbles that lined the stream-bed; it was just as Mora had said—there were plenty of them, and they'd be useful, both as musket-shot and also if he needed to mix mortar—maybe he should think about building a solid barn for the animals, once he got the mining operation underway. He used to be quite good at setting-up structures, and he rather enjoyed the challenge of planning it all out.

First things first, though; he should plan a discreet visit to the British garrison at Gibraltar, so as to get in touch with his old commander. He'd explain the situation, and hope that he still had a shred of credibility left with the man—he'd ask for a loan of manpower, and then get on with the hard work ahead.

CHAPTER 12

Tremaine returned to the homestead in a much better frame of mind, compounded by the fact he could smell that Mora was cooking-up the *paella*. As he sat at the table, he looked about and noted, "The raiders didn't make much of a mess."

"They took some food, and your whiskey," she informed him.

"Did they find your stockpile of weapons?"

"No," she replied, and offered nothing further.

Which was of interest, because where ever this stockpile was, it was hidden from sight—under the floorboards, perhaps? But he didn't see any indication that she'd gone to any lengths to check on it—in fact, the place looked remarkably undisturbed, for having hosted a gang of outlaws.

He offered, "I want to thank you again—the

potion that knocked me out was a godsend; it saved me a rough couple of days."

With an expert flick of her wrist, she flipped the *paella* over. "You must not drink the whiskey any more. In my home country, they believe that such spirits are the work of the devil."

Diplomatically, he replied, "I suppose that's one way of looking at it."

She glanced over at him, curious. "Do you drink the whiskey to forget?"

Since her interest seemed genuine, he decided to answer honestly. "No—I just like the way it makes me feel." He paused. "Although I saw some terrible things during the war—and lost some good friends. I suppose that's all a part of wanting to feel better." And since he was being honest, he confessed, "I know it's not good for me; I've tried to stay sober before, but I could never do it for very long."

She eyed him thoughtfully, as she walked over to distribute the egg dish. "I do not think there is a Lisabetta—she would not let you become so unhappy. A man like you must be brought to bed often, so that you do not think too much."

He chuckled at her plain-speaking, and admitted, "There is a Lisabetta, but she's already married. In fact, she's a bit like you—I wouldn't trust her an inch."

"You can trust me," Mora paused to declare, clearly affronted.

"I will have to, if we are to be married." Since this was a subject foremost in his mind, he decided he'd do a bit of probing, under the guise of joking-about. "I'm just grateful that you didn't murder me, once you found out about the gold. It would have been easy—one more corpse to salt away in the caves." As he took another bite, he watched her from under his brows.

"I would not kill you," she protested in her matter-of-fact tone. "You will be my husband."

He cocked his head, chewing thoughtfully. "I've the feeling there's more to you than you are willing to show."

"This is true," she readily agreed as she seated herself. "But you can trust me."

He paused to smile, genuinely amused. "You are so—so cool-as-ice; like no girl I've ever met."

She glanced at him, as she took a bite. "There was no girl you wished to marry?"

"No."

She considered him for a moment, eying him up and down with a dispassionate gaze. "This is hard for me to believe."

"It's the truth, though. Although I was tempted by a milliner, once."

At her puzzled look, he explained, "It means a

girl who makes hats. I thought perhaps she was a candidate, but then she married someone else." He added in a dry tone, "Someone with a bit more standing."

"Then she was a fool, this girl. You are a good man."

He teased, "I thought I was a drunkard?"

"No more," she pointed out. "We will go to the town in three days, when you are stronger. We will be married, buy the horses, and buy the lumber for the sloo-box. But we will not buy whiskey."

Hiding his bemusement that their marriage was only one item to be ticked off on her list, he cautioned, "We have to be careful not to spend all the money; shearing season is not for a while."

"I have much money." She didn't even look up, as she took another bite.

He raised his brows, since by all appearances this was not at all the case. "You do?" He then asked, half-jokingly, "Is it hidden away with the weapons?"

"*Si*," she replied evenly.

But this disclosure suddenly raised a warning bell in his mind, and he bent his head to eat, in order to hide his alarm. She'd been helping Tosada with his operation during the war—he'd caught glimpses of her, even though she stayed within the homestead for the most part. And now—now she was readily confessing to a stockpile of weapons and money—a stockpile that she was preserving, since she clearly wasn't spending it on herself. In an offhand manner, he ventured, "Where—exactly—is this stockpile?"

"It is hidden in the barn."

He decided he may as well ask outright, "Are you keeping it for the *Afrancesados*?"

"No," she replied, and seemed completely unfazed by the question.

He had no idea whether he should believe her, and he decided to do a bit of pressing—Lord, he always seemed to be on his back foot when it came to her, mainly because he couldn't be certain what she was thinking—she was very hard to read.

Bluntly, he observed, "I think it is strange that these raiders did not steal your chickens."

There was a small silence as she raised her brows, considering this. "They stole the horses."

"But the chickens were also there for the taking, and it's a strange sort of raider who passes up a chance at fresh meat."

"Then I do not know why," she replied, and returned to her meal. "You must ask them, next time they come."

He watched her. "The dog didn't bark at them."

"No," she agreed. "But he seems very friendly—maybe he does not bark."

"How long have you had him, Mora?"

There was a small silence, whilst she stilled her

hands and met his gaze. Then she suddenly smiled her grave smile. "A long time."

He chuckled, relieved that she'd confessed it. "Why did you pretend you didn't know him? Were you afraid I'd object? I wouldn't—he seems a good fellow. What's his name?"

"Sahim," she informed him. "His name is Sahim."

"Sahim." He repeated the word, trying to match her clipped pronunciation. "Does it mean anything?"

She smiled slightly. "It means 'arrow,' in my language."

"Then it's an apt name—he runs like an arrow."

"*Si,*" she agreed. "It is an apt name."

CHAPTER 13

*A*nd so, a few days later—and after the long trek down the mountain on foot—Tremaine found himself standing beside Mora before the local priest at the town's small church, promising to have and to hold so long as they both shall live.

They'd been lucky, since priests tended to ride a circuit in these remote areas, but they'd managed to catch the clergyman while he was in staying in town. Or at least, that's what Señora Frasco told them; she was the local widow who looked after the Padre when he was in residence, and was one of those capable women who helped to plan the rituals of life for the inhabitants of her town.

The señora also stood as the witness for their ceremony—a simple, straightforward affair, mainly because they'd surprised the Padre at his late-afternoon siesta.

"You are an honest man," the priest remarked afterward, shaking Tremaine's hand. "I do not know that another would have married her."

Since Tremaine couldn't very well explain that he was more interested in securing the land than in making an honest woman of Mora, he only nodded and made no comment. And small blame to the priest for making the obvious assumption; Tremaine had been living under the same roof with Tosada's widow, and the townspeople would easily conclude that Mora had set-out to seduce the rather naïve Englishman—by all appearances, it wasn't much of a leap.

She hadn't, of course—which was unexpected in itself. He'd actually thought about this subject on the long trek down the mountain, with Mora being her usual untalkative self. On the one hand, she'd made that comment about how he was the type of man who should be often brought to bed, but on the other hand, she'd never engaged in the slightest hint of alluring behavior. As always, she was something of an enigma, and he wondered what their wedding night held in store.

"You must sign the marriage lines," the priest advised, as he returned to his nap. "Señora Frasca will draw them up."

The older woman dutifully produced a parchment and quill, and as she sat to begin this task, she gave Tremaine a sidelong glance. "This is very sudden, señor."

"It certainly is," Tremaine agreed with a smile, since he knew better than to give the woman a tale to tell—here was a gossip, if he'd ever seen one.

With an arch look, she offered, "Señor Sanchez will be very disappointed."

Despite this innuendo, Tremaine had not caught the sense that the mercantile agent was at all interested in Mora—instead, she seemed to make him nervous. Nevertheless, he humored the older woman by leaning in to whisper, "The poor fellow missed his chance, then," and the señora chuckled in appreciation.

Mora was called over to sign the document, and indicated without a shred of self-consciousness that she didn't know how to sign her name.

As the señora showed her to how to make a mark, Tremaine silently considered this latest piece of the puzzle that was his new bride. It shouldn't be a surprise that she was uneducated, but for some reason he was nonetheless surprised; he already knew she was much more clever than she appeared.

Not to mention there was that persistent suspicion in the back of his mind that she'd been entrusted with Tosada's operation after he'd died—it would readily explain the stockpile of weapons and money that was hidden in the barn. But Napoleon was nothing if not efficient, and the fact that she couldn't write messages or keep accounts seemed to argue against that theory.

With some reluctance, he recognized that he was fighting very hard not to acknowledge what seemed more and more obvious; there would be no reason to preserve the stockpile from Tosada's operation unless Mora was waiting for Napoleon's return, and planned on supplying his soldiers again. It was entirely plausible—it would explain why she'd continued living there alone, for instance. Not to mention that he'd the sense—he'd the sense that the people they met seemed to know something that he didn't.

But then again, this very logical conclusion could be undermined by any number of counter-indicators; unlikely that such an important responsibility would be given to Tosada's foreign widow—an illiterate young woman who'd not been long in the country.

And then there was the fact that she'd no qualms about allowing him to acquire the homestead by marriage, which would obviously throw a spanner into any upcoming supply-train operation. The last needful thing, one would think, was to have a former British officer underfoot if the *Afrancesados* wanted to start it up, again.

And finally, there was the biggest counter-indicator of all; she'd nursed him through a miserable few days rather than simply add his corpse to her collection. After all, no one knew that he was here, and no one would miss him.

Of course, he'd the sense that she rather liked him —the same as he rather liked her—although he had to be careful not to let that cloud his judgment. She was gradually letting her guard down—and they'd had a few semi-honest conversations, although in a strange way, those conversations had left him with more questions than answers.

None of it made much sense, which should stand as a huge warning-flag, in itself. He'd be cautious in his future dealings with her, but one consideration superseded all others; regardless of what her allegiances might be, she held the deed to property that might be important—God willing—to the British cause, and now, with the marriage lines signed and sealed, he'd secured it for himself.

After thanking the Padre and Señora Frasco, the newlyweds emerged from the door of the church into the fading sunlight. "You make a beautiful bride," Tremaine said gallantly, and leaned to kiss Mora on the cheek, since it seemed an appropriate gesture.

"I cannot make hats," she replied with her dry smile. "But I can help you with your gold."

"You mustn't say anything to anyone about the

gold," he cautioned in a low voice, as he glanced around them. "We're not in any shape to defend ourselves—not yet. We'll have to hire a few men, once we get the process started."

"I know men who can help," she offered.

"It has to be people we can trust," he warned.

"*Si*," she insisted. "They are men from my home country—they work in Cadiz."

Cadiz was the closest port on the Mediterranean, and very near Gibraltar. He nodded agreement, even as he knew that he'd be a fool to hire Moroccans to work on a Spanish gold mine; instead, he'd no doubt that his former commander—once informed of the situation—would send security. It would be well-worth the manpower; the war had been at a high cost, and England was scrambling to fund the next round as the diplomats dragged things along at the Congress in Vienna. The victorious allies had convened in that city to work-out the future of Europe, blithely ignoring the fact that Napoleon was threatening again, and all their plans could very well be for naught.

A secret gold mine would be a godsend, right now, and it was doubly a godsend that—with any luck—they could keep it secret. The homestead was in a remote place, and since they were near Cadiz, it would be a simple thing to ship the gold—surreptitiously—wherever it was most needed, or even carry it on horseback though the pass, which would be an ironic twist, all in all.

He considered how best to accomplish the next step, which was to inform his old commander of the potential mining operation. He'd have to travel to Gibraltar, where the British garrison was, and ask to be put in contact—he dared not give a message to anyone else. But unfortunately, he'd a huge credibility problem; hopefully the man would be willing to spare him five minutes of his time—although he hardly deserved it, after all he'd put him through.

And he'd have to think of an excuse to leave Mora behind—he'd come up with something, since there was always the chance that—despite all the counter-indicators—she was working with the *Afrancesados*.

Since it was coming dusk, Tremaine advised, "Once we buy the horses and lumber, it will be too late to climb back up the mountain. I'll ask for a room at the inn tonight, if that's agreeable; it's our wedding night, and we should have a nice meal and do it up proper."

She nodded, "*Si*. If you tell me what is needed, I will buy the lumber from Señor Sanchez—you are better to buy the horses."

This seemed a good plan, and he nodded. "Right; we'll meet back at the inn, then. Let me give you some money."

"I will give *you* some money," she corrected, and pulled a small purse out of her apron pocket. With her grave smile, she handed it to him. "It is my dowry."

"I will pay you back, when I am able," he replied in a firm tone. "But I do appreciate the contribution."

They parted on their errands, and he thought with some amusement that he may have landed himself an unexpected wife, but she definitely had her merits. Assuming, of course, that she wasn't an *Afrancesado* and bent on crossing him up, somehow; the whole situation was more than a little smoky. But on the other hand, they did seem to get along—they were very compatible, despite their differing backgrounds; in many ways, she was as comfortable as an old shoe.

She didn't look like an old shoe, of course, and he was rather looking forward to his wedding night—it had been awhile since he'd been with a woman, and he didn't have the sense she'd need a lot of coaxing.

He set about his errands—finding two horses at the livery stable, along with a mule and a wagon to haul the lumber up the mountain. The animals were nothing to boast about, but beggars couldn't be choosers, in this remote area, and at least they looked sturdy enough for what was needed.

After bargaining over the price, he pulled-out the purse Mora had given him only to find that it contained francs—French coins. After asking the proprietor if he accepted francs—which he did, currencies had a tendency to intermingle after the last war—he decided that it wasn't so very ominous; if the raiders Mora had killed were former *Afrancesados,* then it wouldn't be a surprise that she'd robbed them of francs instead of pesetas. On the other hand, if her stockpile was awaiting Napoleon's return, then francs would be the order of the day.

I hope I'm not being foolish, he thought, as he made his way to the inn with his new wagon and horses. Although if someone had told me a month ago that I'd be here today, married, and owning a fine-looking property—not to mention holding a purseful of French francs—I'd have never believed it. But nevertheless, here I am—everything seems to have fallen into place, and perhaps I should be a bit more optimistic than I am. I wish I could shake the sense that I'm watching an elaborate play—only I don't know, as yet, whether it's a tragedy or a comedy.

CHAPTER 14

A few hours later, Tremaine's mood had improved considerably as he lay drowsy and content in the inn's best room, with Mora asleep beside him.

Their wedding night had all gone well, with minimal awkwardness—which was to be expected, he supposed, considering how matter-of-fact she was about everything else. She was clearly experienced—which was only to be expected, after having been married twice—but on the other hand, she didn't seem to be prostitute-level experienced, which was something of a relief.

All in all, he felt they would rub along together well—as long as she wasn't scheming some scheme that would require him to turn her in, of course. It was a shame, that he couldn't completely trust her, but due to the nature of his past work he was not one to trust anyone—save his former colleagues, of course.

With a mental grimace, he considered what they'd say if they knew about his current situation—and his hole-in-corner marriage, which was the necessary result of that situation. If there was ever an incentive to right his ship, it was the memory of how they'd been so disappointed in him, despite their heartfelt offers of help. Theirs was dangerous work—work that relied on everyone's protecting each other—and he'd failed at it; he'd failed, and let everyone down.

Although he wouldn't be ashamed to have them meet Mora—she was just the sort of woman who'd appeal to them. In fact, he should introduce her to his old commander as a potential operative—she was clever and ruthless, and handy with a weapon. She would not be able to pass for British, of course, but she could pass for a variety of other nationalities; Spanish, Italian, Greek—she could be very useful to the British cause, if the war were to start up again. He wondered whether she spoke other languages—her Spanish was very good, and she seemed to know some English, even though they spoke Spanish to one another. He should test it out, to see.

Hard on this thought, he felt her move, slowly and carefully so as not to wake him. Suddenly alert, he lay still and continued to feign sleep; something in the way she moved told him she was not just getting up to use the necessary, and he listened intently, mentally tensing for action. Despite everything, he still had that instinct that had saved his life on many an occasion—the ability to sense when another person was not acting in his best interests.

Softly—even though he was listening carefully, Tremaine could barely hear her—she slipped out the door on bare feet, and closed it quietly behind her.

Almost immediately, he rolled out of bed and positioned himself low on the wall, his body responding almost automatically to a possible ambush—she might be leaving so that a gunman could come in. Fully alert, he quickly pulled his pistol off the bedside table and watched the door, waiting. He'd have the advantage, since anyone coming in would be silhouetted in the doorway, and therefore an easy target.

No one came in, though. After a few tense moments, he sidled over to the window to lift the curtain with his pistol's muzzle, gazing down into the street below. Nothing. After testing the window sash, he found that it opened with just the barest of squeaks, and so he climbed onto the sill, and pulled himself up over the edge of the roof—not as easy as it used to be, he was still a bit weak.

Carefully spreading his weight over the shingles

so as to make as little noise as possible, he crept up the roof to its peak, to get a better view of the area. There—over by the inn's stables, he could see Mora in the shadows, speaking to two men—or three, it seemed; it was a quarter-moon, and rather dark. But he was certain it was Mora—there was no mistaking the dog who lay at her feet, which was another odd thing; they'd left the dog behind, when they'd come down to the town.

Straining to see in the dark, he watched the shadowy figures. It didn't bode well; the men she met with seemed like tough customers—wiry, and rough-looking—and he wondered if they were remnants from Tosada's operation. Which made it almost certain that she was meeting with them to discuss the gold-mining operation—they'd be licking their chops at the possibility.

But even as he pressed his mouth into a grim line, he noted something unusual; in his former business, he'd learned to watch interactions—to see which person in the group appeared to be in control—and surprisingly, it seemed to him that it was Mora. The men listened intently to what she said without speaking much, and the third one in the shadows reached down to give the dog a quick pat.

She's giving them information, he decided; and again, the secrecy points toward the subject being the potential gold mine—indeed, he could think of no other reason for Mora to scheme behind his back.

He withdrew from the roof's peak, and sidled back toward his window, trying to decide how best to handle this alarming turn of events because—for better or for worse—Mora was now his wife, and he was experiencing a profound sense of disappointment in her betrayal—foolish, since he'd known from the start that she wasn't what she seemed. Best reassess, and make a plan.

The puzzling aspect, of course, was why she hadn't killed him well before now; no one would miss him, after all. Perhaps her plan was to allow him to set-up the mine before he found himself dead in a cave, but on the other hand, that plan didn't make a lot of sense either; his death would not be to her advantage. As she'd already seen, the Spanish laws were not helpful to a wife without children; if he died, the property would wind-up with his family in Wales—which would truly be an ironic end to his sorry saga.

Although—thinking on this—he hit upon a plausible scheme; if she could get pregnant by him, she could secure the land—and the gold mine—for the child. And if that was her plan, then at least he could count on remaining alive until she gave birth.

After lowering himself through the window again, he pulled on his boots with an angry jerk.

Because whatever was brewing, one thing seemed certain; he needed a drink—just a small one, to help fortify him for the coming confrontation. He'd be damned if he was going meekly back to bed—instead, he would hear her answers; she was his wife, after all, and if she was planning to murder him, he'd best find out before they climbed up the mountain again.

CHAPTER 15

And so, when Mora tracked him down it was to find Tremaine at the inn's saloon, having a dram of whiskey and watching the door.

"Tremaine," she scolded, her hands on her hips and thoroughly annoyed. "What do you do?"

"I am waiting for your explanation," he countered. "Who was that you met by the stable?" Hopefully, if she was plotting his murder, a confrontation on the subject would give her pause.

But she didn't seem the least bit fazed, and instead firmly picked up his glass to set it aside. "No more whiskey—not a drop. It is the only way."

"You have not answered my question."

"Not here." She tugged on his arm, and reluctantly, he left the bar to follow her outside—the barkeeper did seem keenly interested in the drama that was unfolding, and he shouldn't have been so indiscreet.

Once they were away from any potential eavesdroppers, she met his gaze with a touch of exasperation. "I meet with the men from my country; I tell them they must help you build your sloo."

With some exasperation, he drew his hand through his hair. "You told someone about the gold? Mora, we are married, now. You can't make such decisions without consulting me."

She stared at him for a long moment, and then nodded in concession. "*Si*—this is true. I am sorry, Tremaine."

"Robert," he corrected, rather distractedly.

"Robert," she agreed.

"All it needs is for these fellows to let it slip—the *guerrillas* have ears everywhere." Indeed, this was a major concern behind the need for secrecy; small chance that the *guerrillas* would stand idly by whilst a Spanish fortune was handed over to the British—and these southern mountains were the *guerrillas*' home turf, so to speak.

"I am sorry, Robert."

Since she seemed genuinely remorseful, he blew out a breath. "Right, then; since they've already been told, I suppose I've little choice but to hope for the best."

"They will help you," she insisted. "They will go

with you tomorrow, up the mountain. They will help you—you will see."

With a frown, he asked, "And where will you be?"

"I will go to the dressmaker." She paused, and then added with a touch of defiance, "I would like to buy new clothes—I am married, now."

This was unexpected; he hadn't paid much attention to her clothes, but it was true that she was a bit ragged, in her well-worn peasant's garb. With a twinge of guilt, he realized he hadn't treated her much like a bride—hadn't even found her a bouquet for their wedding, which made him a sorry excuse for a husband.

On the other hand, if he was any judge of such things, she was the last person on earth who'd linger in town to be fitted for dresses. Not to mention that if her intent had been to recruit her countrymen to assist him, there was no reason to do it in such secrecy. Something was brewing, and he'd best plan accordingly; but damned if he could figure out what it was—she never seemed to be acting consistently.

With a show of feeling guilty—which was what she'd intended, of course—he drew her into a fond embrace and kissed her temple. "Of course, you should arrange for new clothes. Take as long as you like, and keep track of your expenses; I will reimburse you as soon as I am able."

"Thank you, Robert."

"Does the dog come with me, or with you?" he teased as they returned to the inn, walking arm in arm. The animal had appeared—wraith-like—and was trotting along behind them.

"Me," she replied. "He stays with me."

"Take care of our girl," he turned to say to the animal.

She smiled. "Always."

CHAPTER 16

The following morning, Tremaine was introduced to two men who nodded rather tersely upon being introduced, and then said little as they helped him load-up the lumber into the newly-purchased wagon. One climbed into the wagon's seat beside Tremaine, tying his horse to the back, whilst the other rode his horse alongside them as they began the journey up the mountain.

As they rumbled their way up the trail, Tremaine asked the man beside him in a friendly fashion, "Have you ever done any mining?"

"No, Señor," he replied.

"Well, we're going to build a sluice-box, which is a more efficient way to do it than panning the stream. It should also tell us fairly quickly whether the prospect is going to be worth it; if we don't score enough gold over a week or so, then we may have to abandon the idea."

With a casual flick of the reins, he then explained the sluice-box construction whilst the men listened, and took the opportunity to covertly assess his two companions. So far, Mora's story seemed to check-out; since he was familiar with the regional accents found in Spain, he decided almost immediately that these two definitely weren't Spanish—which was a relief, since it meant they weren't *Afrancesados*, intent on doing him in. Instead, they spoke Spanish with the same clipped tones that Mora did—

Suddenly, he stilled. The raiders who'd raided the homestead had spoken in a similar pattern of clipped syllables—was he remembering correctly? Hard to believe that these men had posed as the raiders—unless they were double-crossing Mora, in some way?

Almost immediately, he decided that he was jumping at shadows, again. After all, the raiders had drunk all his whiskey, and these Moroccans wouldn't have touched it. Not to mention that Mora surely would have recognized her own language, in the snatches that they'd managed to hear.

On the other hand—a shame, that there always seemed to be an "other hand"—these two didn't seem to be mere laborers. He was necessarily adept at reading men, and it seemed to him that these two were all business—hard-as-nails, and rather arrogant—which meant they were definitely not inclined to take orders from a woman. But that was the impression he'd garnered last night, whilst watching them from the roof—that they were taking orders from Mora.

Which only reinforced his feeling that he'd best take action, and do a bit of table-turning—he needed to discover the true reason Mora had wanted to stay in town. With this in mind, he looked for a likely spot, as they continued up the trail, and eventually decided upon a rocky outcropping that obscured a copse of trees behind it.

"Let me stop here for a moment," he announced, and tied-up the wagon's reins, pretending that he had to go relieve himself.

He disappeared behind the rock, and after a moment, he shouted to the outrider, "Have a look at this."

The mounted man duly directed his horse around the rocky outcropping, and was caught completely by surprise when Tremaine leapt upon him, yanking him from his horse as he held a pistol to the man's head. "Don't move," he said quietly. "Put your hands up."

After relieving the man of his weapon, Tremaine marched him back to the wagon, where his companion watched them approach with an alarmed expression. "What do you do, *Ingles*? We mean you no harm."

"That's as may be," Tremaine answered fairly. "But something doesn't add up, and I'll be damned if I'll be played for a fool. Throw your weapons down, and hands up."

There was a pause, whilst Tremaine could sense that the two men were communicating silently. "*Si*," the one in the wagon finally agreed, and after tossing his weapon, he raised his hands.

As the others watched, Tremaine mounted his own horse and gathered-up their horses' reins in his hand. "I'll leave your weapons a half-mile down the mountain; I'll set a rock marker."

They made no reply as they watched him quickly move away, leading the two horses behind him; with only the wagon's old mule, they'd have a tough time pursuing him.

As Tremaine made his way down the mountain, he couldn't help but admire the irony of stumbling across a possible enemy operation whilst trying—for once—to mind his own business. If that's what this was, of course—damned if he could make much sense of it. Even though the obvious explanation was that Mora was working with the *Afrancesados*, the major holes in that theory remained—the main one being that she'd allowed someone like him to blunder in, and possibly jeopardize the scheme.

While it was possible that she'd married him with an eye to owning the gold mine through her child, that didn't explain everything; he was completely certain she'd no idea about the gold before he'd let it slip, in his delirium.

So; perhaps she'd tolerated him so as to raise no suspicions, and then—once she learned of the gold—had seized upon the opportunity.

Which was a plausible theory, save that there were a few things that still didn't fit—first among them the extraordinary fact that she'd been willing to nurse him through a rough couple of days before she knew anything about the gold mine. She wasn't the type of woman who would do such a thing out of sheer kindness, especially considering her ready confession that she'd killed a lot of men. He believed her.

It was all very puzzling, but above all he had to remember that—even though they might be working at cross-purposes—she was now his wife; he couldn't treat her the same as he would any other enemy operative.

And here I thought I'd nothing to live for, he thought a bit grimly; save this dubious prospect of gearing-up a gold mine in an effort to redeem myself. And then—lo and behold—I'm thrown right back into the game again.

He found a place to leave the men's weapons—

and tied their horses to a tree, in a gesture of good will—before making his way down the remainder of the mountain. Carefully skirting the town, he found a vantage point where he could watch the main street unseen, and stayed there for the rest of the day.

He didn't see Mora, but it seemed clear to him that she must have stayed behind so as to make contact with someone—she was not one to care about new clothes. If his theory was correct—that she was a French operative of some sort—then she'd have a liaison planted in the town somewhere; this place was too isolated for her to carry her own messages back and forth, and messaging was the life's blood of any operation. And since Señora Frasco had intimated that Mora often spoke privately to the mercantile agent, it gave him a very good guess as to who that liaison must be.

CHAPTER 17

To this end, Tremaine focused his attention upon the mercantile agent's shop, but despite watching the comings and goings carefully, he saw no sign of Mora—nor did he see any sign that the two Moroccan men had returned to town, which was interesting; you'd think they'd want to report to her about his double-dealing, post-haste. Unless they were aware that she was no longer here, which seemed more and more likely, as the day went on without any sign of her.

Since he was fairly certain that Señor Sanchez was Mora's liaison, he waited until day's end, and then as soon as the man went to lock the shop's front door, Tremaine slipped in at the back, and—with a swift move—accosted the agent with a show of force;

banging the portly man hard against the counter, and twisting his arm mercilessly behind him.

"Where's Mora?"

"Ah—I—I do not know, *Ingles*," the agent protested in a panic. "Ay—you hurt me."

Tremaine twisted harder. "Tell me."

The man cried out in pain. "I do not know—I swear."

"Do you know her game?"

"There—there is no game, Señor."

But Tremaine had seen the flare of alarm in his eyes, quickly extinguished, and leaned in to say with deadly intensity, "We can do this the easy way or the hard way. No one will hear you."

He wrenched the man's arm so that he groaned in agony before he managed to gasp, "She—she goes to Cadiz, sometimes."

This rang true; since Cadiz was the nearest port on the Mediterranean, it was entirely plausible that Napoleon's supporters would look for messages there, since the Emperor himself was being held at a nearby island.

Tremaine persisted, "Cadiz is a big place; who does she meet?"

"She meets—I think she meets with the British Colonel, from the garrison."

With a mighty effort, Tremaine hid his extreme alarm. Was Mora infiltrating the British outpost at

Gibraltar? Perhaps it was worse than he thought—perhaps she was what the service called an "angel"—a female agent sent to seduce opposition leaders.

Tremaine eased the pressure on the man's arm and replied with a touch of scorn, "Fah—you're completely useless. The only reason I've come to town is because the British Colonel sent me to give her support."

The man raised his eyebrows. "The Mademoiselle works for the *British*?" he exclaimed in astonishment.

"You didn't hear it from me," Tremaine replied, and gave the man's arm one last wrench before he released him. May as well undermine her credibility with this fellow—it was always useful to sow seeds of distrust amongst the enemy operatives—and it was looking more and more like Mora was one of them; it was a pity, but this fellow's reaction seemed to confirm it. "If you see her, tell her I'm back at the homestead and I must speak with her immediately."

"*Si—si*, Señor."

Tremaine pulled his knife, and displayed it in the man's face. "Say nothing of this, or it will be the worse for you."

"No," the man fervently agreed, clearly relieved that his ordeal appeared to be over. "I will say nothing—my promise, *Ingles*."

This was, of course, very unlikely—this fellow would be in a fever to report Mora's supposed double-dealing to whoever was higher up the *Afrancesado* chain of command. It would be useful to see who this fellow went to meet—Tremaine needed to go to warn the British garrison, anyway, and it would be doubly satisfying tell them about the gold mine as well as expose this nest of *Afrancesados*.

He walked over to the shelves to help himself to a bag of flour—to support his story of returning to the homestead—and for a moment, he struggled with the impulse to take a whiskey bottle, too. Best not; he needed his wits about him. If nothing else, he should be grateful to Mora for putting him on the path to sobriety—it was the strangest twist of all, in this twisted tale, and he should stick with it if he was to have any hope of convincing his old commander that he'd a shred of credibility.

Therefore—after tipping his hat in an ironic gesture—he exited the place, and then swiftly stole away to regain his lookout perch, so as to watch the man's next movements.

CHAPTER 18

As Tremaine had expected, the mercantile agent set off for Cadiz at first light the next morning—casting many a furtive glance around him, and behaving like a man on a mission.

Carefully keeping out of sight, Tremaine trailed him to Cadiz, a journey that brought back memories of his time in the service; often the days were tedious and long, with little to do save watch and wait. And he acknowledged that it wasn't good for him to be alone too long with his thoughts—despite her questionable allegiances, Mora had been right about that. If he'd too much time on his hands, he'd start drinking so as to avoid having his mind obsess over unwelcome memories—his harsh childhood, or the boon companions whose lives had been cut short by a merciless enemy.

On some level, he was aware of this—that he had trouble controlling his thoughts—and it was one of the reasons he'd hit upon this mining scheme; if he was going to succeed without falling back into bad habits, he needed to keep his mind and body focused on a difficult task, so that he was left with little time for reflection.

Funny, that Mora had gained this insight after knowing him just a few days, but on the other hand she was as shrewd as they came—only see how her story kept changing so as to allay his suspicions. And it was interesting that everyone seemed to refer to her as 'the Mademoiselle', even though she wasn't French and had been married at least twice. The use of a *nom de guerre* only supported his suspicion that she was a Napoleonic agent—apparently one who'd decided she rather fancied Robert Tremaine; it was the only explanation as to why she'd behaved with such restraint, and had nursed him through such a miserable time.

And now they were married, and he was going to reward her kindness with a betrayal—but he was overthinking, again, and he should instead focus on what was to happen next; he'd find out who she met with in Cadiz, and then lay it all before his old commander—whose reaction could only be imagined, upon learning that his former agent had managed to marry a French spy, all unknowing.

And despite the fact she was married to him, they'd deal with her harshly—too much was at stake, with Napoleon rattling his saber again. Tremaine could ask for leniency, to try to save her from a swift execution; he did feel an obligation, and he'd grown rather fond of her, truth to tell. But it would be a hard sell; he'd little grace left with the service, and they may not be inclined to grant him any favors.

Whilst he entertained these rather heavy thoughts, he followed Sanchez into Cadiz, where the man made his way to the town's busy docks and into a rather seedy taverna—the type of place where sailors would look for a bit of entertainment when in port. No surprise, of course; all the operatives from the last war—and from every side—used busy port towns to stage operations, since merchant-ship activity served as a plausible cover for transport and messaging.

The mercantile agent took a long look around, and then ducked into the taverna's low entry door as Tremaine lingered across the street, pretending to smoke a cheroot and keeping the brim of his hat low across his face. He watched the comings and goings for a few minutes—it was always dangerous to enter an establishment without first doing a thorough reconnoiter—and it was a shame that he didn't have a partner to position at the back entrance.

Therefore, it was with some astonishment that he

observed a sailor, approaching the entry door with a rolling sailor's gait—only it wasn't a sailor at all; the man may be able to fool others, but Tremaine was well-familiar with the angle of his jaw and the set of his shoulders. The sailor was his former commander.

After recovering from his astonishment, he arrived at the logical conclusion with a sense of acute dismay; a trap was being set. If Sanchez was an enemy operative, it was no coincidence that his former spymaster was entering into the same taverna at the same time. Throwing down his cheroot, Tremaine assessed the passersby as he approached the entry with firm strides—he'd provide support, or at least create a diversion so as to allow his commander to escape.

But—thinking along these lines—he paused for a moment, as he hovered on the threshold. There was always the possibility that the spymaster was well-aware of what was going forward—he was a shrewd player in his own right—and he may have disguised himself to listen-in on whatever conversations Sanchez was to have with whoever was posted within. If Tremaine charged-in like the calvary, he might bungle the operation.

Coming to a decision, he casually entered through the door as though he'd nothing more on his mind than snatching a quick drink; he'd monitor the situation without giving away his commander's role, and give assistance only if it seemed necessary.

The taverna was busy this time of day, with many a dockman coming off his shift and looking for mates and female companionship. Tremaine watched his spymaster wade through the throng as he made his way toward the crowded bar, where Señor Sanchez had already elbowed himself into a spot.

Tremaine hovered near the back, and watched his commander's casual movements—movements which were belied by the man's sharp gaze. He's wary, Tremaine decided, and tried to determine whether he should make his presence known; he didn't see any familiar faces running protection for the man, but it strained credulity to think he'd come in here all alone, and without support.

Whilst he tried to decide his next move, he manuevered toward the center of the room so as to get a better view, and then was astonished to behold Mora's dog—Sahim—leaning against the foot of the bar, and looking as though he wasn't enjoying the crowded environment. With a quick, keen gaze, Tremaine searched for the dog's mistress, but the only women in the place were the barmaids serving drinks, and the prostitutes flirting with the clientele.

Tremaine brought his gaze back to the dog just in time to see the barkeeper lean down to pat him with a casual gesture, and in the movement, Tremaine realized that the barkeeper was the third man who'd met with Mora beside the stables.

With this alarming development, Tremaine felt he'd no choice but to show himself—it was looking more and more like a trap. Shouldering others aside, Tremaine pushed his way forward until he squeezed into the bar next to Sanchez, putting his back to the spymaster. Squarely confronting the barkeeper, he drew his pistol, resting it covertly on the counter.

"Hold, he addressed the man, lifting the weapon slightly so that he could see it. "Keep your hands on the counter."

With a show of surprise, the barkeeper turned his palms. "Señor—what is this?"

"He is an enemy operative," Tremaine said in English, without looking at the spymaster.

"Is he?" the spymaster replied in the same language. "You astonish me."

But any further conversation was halted when Señor Sanchez suddenly stood upright, staring at Tremaine and blustering in astonishment. "You! What do *you* do here?"

But he wasn't to say anything further, on this day or any other, because his eyes suddenly widened in horror as he collapsed to the floor. Behind him stood Mora, and Tremaine caught a quick glimpse of a bloody stiletto before it disappeared into her apron pocket.

"Stand down," the spymaster cautioned him quietly in English.

But Tremaine didn't need to be told, having already done a bit of surprised reassessing.

The barkeeper gazed down at the fallen man with an expression of resigned amusement. "Fellow's drunk," he declared. He nodded to one of the workers, who immediately bent to hoist the corpse over his shoulder, and disappear with it into the back room.

There were a few chuckles, but the crowd generally ignored the interruption—such a thing was commonplace, after all—and Tremaine bent his head as though he didn't recognize his wife, leaving a coin on the counter for the barkeeper before he turned away; he'd follow his orders to stand down.

Mora, however, wasn't having it. "Robert," she chided crossly, as she confronted him before he could melt back into the crowded room. "What do you do here? Only see what you have done."

"Careful," said the spymaster in Spanish, as he idly contemplated his drink.

"It is you, who should be careful," she retorted. "Is this your doing?"

"It is not," the spymaster replied.

Mora turned to Tremaine. "Where are my men?"

"I would like to know what's going on," Tremaine replied steadily, including both the spymaster and

Mora in this request. "I don't appreciate being duped."

With an annoyed gesture, she threw up her hands. "Fah—there is no 'duped'; why did you not go back to the homestead?"

"I'm sure he meant well," the spymaster offered in a meek tone.

"You will keep quiet," Mora directed in a cutting tone. "You must leave, now; there has been enough damage done."

But the Englishman only eyed Tremaine over the edge of his glass. "I understand there is a gold mine at play."

"Yes, sir," Tremaine answered readily. "There is definitely gold in the mountain, but it remains to be seen whether it would be profitable to mine it."

"Very well," the spymaster replied, as he placed his glass on the counter with a click. "Keep me informed."

"Go," Mora repeated.

"Yes—I am *de trop*. Don't release the hound, I beg of you." A glint of amusement appeared in his grey eyes, as he turned away. "I will leave you two to sort it out."

CHAPTER 19

"We will go," Mora directed Tremaine, and then said a few words to the barkeeper in her own language, with the man not looking up or acknowledging her in any way.

Almost without thinking, Tremaine put a protective hand on his wife's back to escort her through the crowd, and couldn't help but notice that—while most paid little attention to them—several men quickly moved out of their path, their expressions quickly averted.

They're afraid of her, Tremaine realized; she's "the Mademoiselle" but she's not French, and she doesn't work for Napoleon—unless my old commander has completely lost his bearings. But whoever she is, she's as handy with a blade as she is with a musket, and I am the current husband—the previous two having met swift deaths.

These rather alarming thoughts were interrupted when they emerged into the evening air—infused with the smell of the sea—and she chided with no small exasperation, "Robert; why did you not do as you were told?"

But he was not going to be scolded, and answered steadily, "I knew something was off, Mora, and it made me wary. You should have trusted me."

"You did not trust me," she countered.

This was only fair, and he acknowledged, "I'm sorry—but I was worried you were an *Afrancesado*. Señor Sanchez certainly thought you were."

She pressed her lips together in annoyance. "*Si*, and now he is no longer alive to tell others such a thing."

He was silent as they walked a few paces down the street. So—he'd unwittingly destroyed a useful dupe for her, and again he said, "I'm sorry, but I wish I'd been better informed."

She eyed Tremaine in remonstrance. "Were you seen with him?"

"No—I'm not that clumsy. No one will connect me with his disappearance."

She lifted her brows and nodded in satisfaction. "Good. At least you did not make that mistake."

"Be fair, Mora—I knew that you were lying to me,

and that I'd best find out why. You should have trusted me—there would have been no harm in telling me you were working for the British."

For whatever reason, this seemed to amuse her, and in a strange way it broke the tension between them. "I do not work for the British."

This gave him pause, but—on second thought—shouldn't have been much of a surprise, since she'd behaved as though she was on an equal footing with the spymaster; she definitely didn't regard him as her superior. "Who do you work for, then? And why were you meeting with—with that British sailor?" He should be careful what he disclosed; if she was not working for the spymaster, she may not even know his true identity.

She didn't answer for a few moments as they walked along the dock, and he could sense she was contemplating how best to answer. He put a hand on her back again, and insisted, "I'm your husband, Mora. We should try to be honest with each other, or this marriage is never going to work."

As though coming to a decision, she stopped to face him. "Very well, Robert; I will tell you. But first, let us go to a better place."

With a soft whistle, she summoned the dog, who emerged from the shadows and immediately took-up his usual place, following at a small distance behind them.

CHAPTER 20

They walked out to the end of a pier, where they would be quite alone, and then she settled onto a pile of nets, indicating with a gesture that he should sit beside her.

The ocean breeze was a bit chilly, and so he offered, "Shall I give you my coat? Are you cold?"

"I am always cold," she answered readily, as she accepted the offer. "It is not like my country."

He sat beside her in his shirtsleeves, and they were silent for a few moments. He thought—she is trying to decide whether or not to tell me the truth, I think. She's an expert at keeping her own counsel—that much is obvious—and I imagine she gives information out very, very sparingly. But I also think—despite everything that's happened—that she tends to tell the truth, which is rather a surprise. She may have shaded the truth so as to mislead me, but nevertheless I think she's forthright, in her own way. It's in keeping with her fearlessness—only see how she didn't hesitate to scold the spymaster, which is something even the bravest of our men wouldn't have dreamed of doing—not to mention she'd no problem doing so in a public place. She's just that bold.

So as to give her a place to start, he asked, "Tell me about how you came to meet—to meet the sailor?"

"It was the Englishman who asked to meet with me," she answered. "I was here in Cadiz, during the war." She smiled, slightly. "Many ships, coming and going."

He frowned slightly. "Did your husband work here, at the docks?"

"No," she replied. "Instead, I worked here with my men. The Englishman wished my help for his war—help from me and my men."

This was rather surprising, and he frowned. "He recruited men from *Morocco*?"

"*Si*," she agreed, a bit amused by his incredulity. "Men from my country, who like to cause trouble for those who cause trouble for others. Brave men, with swift horses and swifter boats."

Realization hit, and he lifted his brows. "Your men are pirates."

"*Si*," she agreed. "Pirates."

He was silent for a moment, realizing that he probably should have guessed this before now. Piracy had been an honorable profession in Morocco for centuries, and it only made sense that a band of them had taken advantage of the chaos of war, and had targeted the supply ships for looting. What was unexpected was that a female had decided to take-up such a profession, and had apparently been successful enough to catch the attention of the British spymaster.

Piecing it together, he guessed, "He asked you to disrupt Napoleon's suppliers? Target their ships, in particular?"

"No, Robert," she explained patiently, as she gathered his coat a bit closer around her. "He asked us to go to the homestead."

He held her gaze for a moment, and then slowly shook his head. "I don't understand—you were working with Tosada, at the homestead; I saw it myself—it was a way-station for the *Afrancesados*."

"We killed Tosada," she informed him bluntly. "And then one of my men took his place."

In some surprise, he stared at her. "And no one noticed?"

"No one noticed," she affirmed. "The suppliers who came through would not suspect."

He could only admire the ingeniousness of it—no one would imagine that the British had infiltrated

Napoleon's way-station—and suddenly it made sense, that the spymaster would recruit foreigners for the task; if he used local men, there was always the danger that the *Afrancesados* might recognize them. Not to mention these lot were pirates, and would already know how to run such an operation flawlessly.

"And?" he asked, fascinated.

She lifted a shoulder. "We ambushed the suppliers, and then my men would take the places of the dead men, and deliver the supplies over the pass to the supply trains." She smiled her grave smile. "Only now, the muskets would jam, and the black powder was mixed with ashes."

"You tainted the supplies." He paused in admiration. "Good Lord. And they never caught on?"

"There was always a different supply train, moving through to receive the goods," she explained. And so, my men would ride back over the pass, and do it all over again."

"Amazing," he breathed in admiration. "And yet, such a simple, bold plan."

"It worked well," she agreed, in her matter-of-fact way.

"How many bodies are in the caves?"

"Many," she replied. "We must move them somewhere else, if they are in the way of the gold."

Unable to help himself, he started to laugh—Lord,

it had been a long time since he'd laughed. "Good Lord, Mora; I think it's probably a good thing you decided not to be a nun."

"*Si*," she agreed. "And I cannot make hats, like the sweet girl you wished to marry."

This, said rather tartly—it seemed she was a little jealous of her unknown rival—and so as to soothe her, he said, "You mustn't fling that at me—it meant nothing. And surely, you've had someone catch your fancy, along the way?"

Promptly, she answered, "*Si*—the man who smuggled me out of Algiers." Thinking this over, she shrugged. "It was to be expected; I was young, and he was handsome—and oh, so very brave."

Fascinated by this glimpse, he ventured, "But he turned you down?"

"He is a man of God," she explained. "He is not one for women—especially a woman like me, who did not think it was a sin to kill those who deserve it. And so, I decided that I will help him, instead." She met his eyes, very seriously. "This is what I do, Robert; I do not care who wins your wars. I help a group of men smuggle slave girls from Algiers to France, so that they may be free."

"The Knights of Malta," Tremaine guessed, since he'd heard rumors.

"I will not say," she replied evenly.

He nodded in understanding. The Knights were a

Roman Catholic religious order that had absorbed the Knights Templar when that group was forcibly disbanded, centuries ago. The Order were known to be at the forefront in fighting slavery, and so her story made a great deal of sense.

She continued, "Money is always needed for this—for ships, and to bribe the guards. So, I send them money—much money." She paused. "The man in Algiers, he is very honorable, and he would not accept the money if he knew it was stolen from dead men. And so, the Englishman agreed that he would take my francs and exchange them for English money, to be sent to Algiers. Since the money comes from the English, the holy man in Algiers thinks it is clean money, and not blood-money."

Tremaine whistled softly. "That's extraordinary."

She shrugged again. "Me and my men, we do not care about England, or Spain, or which fat man sits on which throne. But we know that where there is war, there is much money to be seized."

He nodded, because it had suddenly occurred to him why he'd been assigned to keep an eye on the homestead, during the war; no doubt his spymaster was not completely certain he could trust these lawless Moroccans to do as they'd promised. But they had—because they weren't doing it for themselves; their cause was more important than riches to them. Leave it to a band of pirates, to appreciate the importance of freedom.

So; this strange tale was finally falling together, but there was one portion of it that continued to puzzle him. "I think it was your men, who raided the homestead when—when I was sick."

"*Si*," she said easily. "I asked them to take the horses and the whiskey."

Puzzled, he shook his head slightly. "I don't understand, though—why?"

With a small shrug, she confessed, "The Englishman, he tells me—this Tremaine is a good man, but I had to let him go because he drinks too much whiskey. And now he wishes to go back to your mountain and live alone, which will be very bad for him because he thinks too much. If you can cure him of his bad habit and put him to work, I will pay you well."

For a long moment, Tremaine stared at her, bereft of speech. So; his spymaster had arranged for this—this situation, knowing he'd be isolated with a hard taskmaster who was not going to put up with any relapses. One last chance had been given him—anonymously, of course; that was how the man operated. In a strange way, it made him feel almost ashamed.

Quietly, he said, "Thank you for telling me this, Mora."

Her eyes slid to his. "Do not tell him I said."

"No. but I am grateful to the both of you."

She quirked her mouth. "But then you tell me, in your spirits-sickness, that you are not there to raise sheep, you are there to take gold from the mountain. It made me think—I must help this man do this. The holy man in Algiers would be so pleased to have this gold, and I am tired of having nothing to do."

"It is the British, who will need the gold," he corrected her rather firmly. "They will need it to fight Napoleon again."

She lifted a shoulder. "What the British want does not matter to me."

"It matters a lot to me, though, and I'm your husband."

With a "tsking" sound, she replied, "You must not worry, Robert; I have struck a deal with the Englishman. If there is gold, we will divide it up the same way we divide up the French francs. I do not wish to make an enemy of him, and he does not wish to make an enemy of me. And he is pleased to help the holy men in Algiers, I think—even though they are not of his church."

Tremaine could see the wisdom of this decision, and couldn't resist pointing out, "You may not care who wins these wars, Mora, but it's helped your cause that the British are gaining control of so much of the world. We've been at the forefront in trying to abolish slavery, and—now that we have so much influence—things are finally starting to change."

But her response surprised him, as she shook her head rather gravely. "No, Robert; there will always be slavery—as long as there are young girls and powerful men." Nodding to herself, she gazed out over the ocean. "But we work to save one life at a time, and maybe we are killed, and maybe we are not." She glanced at him with a small, indulgent smile. "You think the world will change, but you are not hard, like me."

"I suppose," he slowly agreed. "You have the better insight on the topic, certainly. Perhaps we will rub off on each other—you'll be softer, and I'll be harder."

"*Si*," she agreed, clearly pleased by this idea. "And now we have had enough talk, and it is time to go to bed."

CHAPTER 21

The following morning, he was lying in bed and idly watching Mora as she washed herself at the bedstand. They were becoming accustomed to each other, and he had to admit that there was much to be said for having a wife, when it came to bed-sport. No need, any longer, to look for a willing woman who was not a prostitute; Mora was definitely willing, and unashamed to show that she was willing. But even during lovemaking, he'd the sense that she remained very self-contained—the past events in her life had created an impenetrable inner-fortress, and he acknowledged that the two of them probably would never be on an intimate footing, the way some of his old cohorts were with their wives.

She was very different from them—and unlike

any woman he'd ever met, even though he'd met more than a few hardened women, in his business. Nearly always, he'd sensed that their hardness was a façade to hide the fact that they were vulnerable, beneath their bravado. But Mora was different—he didn't get the sense that she wore her attitude like a protective shield. Instead, she was hardened like a lot of men that he knew—practical and stoic, rather than trying to hide her vulnerabilities. And he did get the sense that she was fond of him—in the same way that he was fond of her. Theirs was no love-match, but there was something to be said about having a wife who was so forthright—there would be no guessing about how she felt.

Of course, it was possible that his old commander was still paying her to keep an eye on him—but it seemed very unlikely that she'd agree to anything that she didn't wish to do. It rather tied-in to what she'd told him; she was fatalistic, and took life as it came—and currently, she was satisfied to be married to a disgraced British operative.

I may never have another drink, he realized, surprised by the very idea. I may not be allowed—and I suppose that was the whole point of this exercise. I'm to be given a hard cure, to see if there is any hope for me.

Mora turned to him, as she dried herself off with

a towel. "You must rise, Robert; we visit the gypsy camp, today."

He raised his brows. "We do?"

"*Si*. The Englishman says we must take a gypsy man back to the mountain to test the gold, to see if it is good. We cannot trust anyone in San Ysidro to do this, and he says he can't trust the Spanish *guerrillas*, either—he has learned this lesson."

Tremaine tended to agree with this assessment—the *guerrillas* were worthy allies when they wanted to be, but they would betray the British without a moment's hesitation if it came down to what was best for Spain.

With some skepticism, he noted, "I'm not sure we can trust the gypsies any more than we can trust the *guerrillas*."

"It is best to trust no one," she agreed. "But he says we must know if the trouble will be worth it, and he says this gypsy man owes him his life."

"Very well, then. The Romanies tend to have decent horses—maybe we can trade mine for a better one."

"There are no horses like the ones in my country," she advised with a great deal of regret. "But we can hope."

It was evident that she'd met-up with his old commander before the confrontation at the taverna, and so he asked, "How do you communicate with the Englishman? Do you have a liaison in San Ysidro?"

"I do not say," she said evenly, as she lowered her blouse over her head.

He raised his brows in surprise. "Even to me?"

She shook her head slightly, as she began to braid her hair. "Even to you. Many have spoken of such things, and many are dead."

The words hung in the air, and unspoken was the inarguable fact that—at present, at least—he was something of a weak link. To cover the awkwardness, he teased, "Sahim runs messages, I'll bet."

"Sometimes," she agreed, in all seriousness.

Since she wasn't going to tell him what he wished to know, he decided to change the subject. "Sahim is from Morocco too, I think."

"*Si*," she agreed. With a small gleam, she glanced his way, as she wound her scarf around her head. "He has met you, before."

Again, he raised his brows in surprise. "He has? I don't think so—I'd remember him; he's very unusual-looking."

She turned back for one last look in the mirror, as she tied her apron behind her. "At the homestead, when you were spying on us. I told Sahim to let me know if you came too close—I did not want the *Afrancesados* to become suspicious."

With mixed emotions, he stared at her. "You knew I was there."

"*Si*. Do not tell the Englishman; it would hurt his feelings."

Still puzzled, he ventured, "But I don't recall seeing Sahim, when I was posted there."

"No," she agreed, and said no more.

It's all rather alarming, he decided, as he rolled out of bed. Between the Moroccans and the *guerrillas*, it seems my spymaster can be easily outfoxed. Which only makes sense, I suppose; their tactics are so different than ours. Perhaps we should take a page—develop some sort of military unit that operates by stealth and sabotage.

Mora interrupted his thoughts. "You must not say why the gypsy comes with us."

He had to chuckle, as he pulled on his boots. "I may be clumsy, but I'm not *that* clumsy."

She smiled in apology, and put a hand on his shoulder. "No. I am sorry, Robert. Indeed, you are very clever; you knew to track Señor Sanchez—I was very much surprised."

But this did not, in fact, make him feel any better. "I blundered in, though, and as a consequence you lost a useful dupe."

But she only continued to smile, as he opened the door for her. "Do not worry; there are many more of the dupes."

"But I suppose you won't tell me who they are."
"No, I will not," she replied, matter-of-factly.

CHAPTER 22

And so, Tremaine found himself riding into the Romany camp, which had been set-up in a quiet area along the Guadalete River; the colorful caravans forming the traditional circle around a central campfire.

He'd never had much contact with Romanies—they were scarce in Wales—but he knew that the European tribes had been decimated during the war. It made sense that they'd have a man who knew how to assay gold, though—the Romanies were known as metalworkers from way back. Hopefully, the man could be trusted; when there was a fortune at stake, people tended to lose their bearings and it seemed the spymaster was taking a chance, in trusting a gypsy with such information. Mora had said the man owed the spymaster his life, but loyalty was something in short supply, nowadays—especially between the factions that had been only tenuously bound together during the war.

They dismounted, and approached the woman who sat tending the fire at the center of the encampment. After silently watching them approach, she turned her head to call out *"Gadjos, Baro,"* and in short order a man emerged from one of the caravans—tall and taciturn, and not exactly overjoyed to see them. Tremaine couldn't help but note that the gypsy chief's gaze rested on Mora for a brief moment before it turned to himself.

"Greetings," Tremaine offered in a cheerful tone. "I'm Robert Tremaine; I believe you may have been expecting us."

His show of friendliness disguised the fact he was carefully assessing his surroundings and gauging the man who stood before them—unlikely it was a trap, but there were some cross-currents here that he couldn't quite like; the gypsies who watched from their caravans were silent, and wary.

They'd no reason to be, if they were willing to volunteer one of their own—but on the other hand, the Romanies notoriously didn't like to be drawn-in to outsider disputes—and with good reason, considering how much they'd suffered during the war.

Although he couldn't help but notice that this particular tribe seemed to be doing well—the wagons had fresh paint, and the children who were playing in the meadow looked well-fed and happy. In addition, there were some fine-looking horses contained in the temporary corral that had been set-up, and Tremaine's gaze rested on a glossy black mare who was cropping at the long grass. She was a good-looking horse—not too big and not too small; sturdy enough for mountain work.

The gypsy chief nodded to him, but didn't offer his hand. "Greetings."

"I understand you will send a worker to help us, back in San Ysidro."

The man nodded. "*Si*." He turned his head, and—with palpable reluctance—an older man stepped forward. "This is Gerard."

With a disarming smile, Tremaine assessed the assayer, and surmised that the man was a brother or cousin to the chief; there was definitely a resemblance, even though Gerard was shorter and older. Which was interesting; you'd think the older male would be the hereditary chief, but maybe the gypsies didn't operate the same way.

Despite the fact that Gerard seemed just as recalcitrant as the *Baro*, Tremaine offered, "Thanks so much for helping us out—appreciate it."

But the older man only regarded him from under sullen brows. "How much will you pay me, *gadjo*?"

For the first time, Mora spoke. "The British will pay you. Do not cheat me, *kafir*."

The words hung in the air—obviously, there was some history between these three—and as the *Baro* lowered his gaze to the ground, Gerard spread his hands and blustered, "Oh? Oh, of course—I was mistaken, then. Many apologies, Mademoiselle."

"Mrs. Tremaine," Tremaine corrected, watching them closely. "This woman is my wife."

At that, both Romany men gazed at him in surprise. They think I've lost my mind, Tremaine realized, which means they know plenty that I don't, and I'd best try to find out what it is.

The older woman at the campfire broke the silence. "Come, Mrs. Tremaine," she offered, with a show of heartiness. "I will fetch a gift for you—a wedding gift, made with my own hands."

"You are very kind," said Mora, and the tension was broken, as she walked over to take a seat by the fire.

"I will fetch my satchel," Gerard told Tremaine. "It will take but a moment."

Seizing the opportunity for private conversation, Tremaine asked the gypsy chief, "Are you willing to do some horse-trading? I wouldn't mind having something more suited for mountain work."

With an expert eye, the *Baro* ran his gaze over Tremaine's animal. "Perhaps. Come this way, *gadjo*."

CHAPTER 23

Tremaine walked with the *Baro* over to the temporary corral, and ventured in an offhand manner, "The black mare looks to be sound." She also looked to be well beyond his means, but there was no harm in putting it to the test.

And as could be expected, his overture was shut down in short order. "The mare is not for sale, *gadjo*."

Tremaine chuckled. "You can't blame me for trying; she's a beauty."

For the first time, the gypsy chief seemed to soften a bit, and he made a gesture with his head toward the other animals. "Come; I will show you the ones I would trade."

As they walked to the end of the corral, Tremaine decided he'd best make the most of the opportunity, and said in an even tone, "I'd appreciate it if you would tell me what you know about my wife. It seems to me that no one here is very happy to see her."

For a long moment, Tremaine wondered if the *Baro* would respond, but then, as they came a halt at the end of the corral, the other man said, "Her dog tried to kill me."

In some surprise, Tremaine stared at him. "The dog tried to *kill* you?"

"*Si*; I had to leap up a tree, and I still bear the scar on my leg."

"Good Lord."

In a dispassionate tone, the man added, "The dog is a killer."

Diplomatically, Tremaine refrained from mentioning that Sahim was somewhere in the vicinity, staying out of sight, and instead asked, "Why did he go after you?"

"They have fine horses, her men; one of my own men was foolish enough to steal one." He paused. "We gave them three of ours, in apology."

This was all very interesting—although Tremaine was already aware that his new bride showed him a side that—apparently—was rarely shown to anyone else; obviously, his old commander hadn't recruited her for her warmth and kindness. All in all, it was more of a shock to hear Sahim thus described, and he admitted, "I'm amazed; the dog seems so friendly."

The Romany man made a derisive sound. "He is known as *Sahim Almawt*—the Arrow of Death. If you see the Arrow, you know to be wary; the Mademoiselle is nearby."

Slowly, Tremaine nodded. "I see. I appreciate the information."

The other man shrugged. "I did not know if you were aware."

Mainly, Tremaine was aware that he shouldn't provide any details, and so he only hedged, "It's all a bit hard to explain, actually."

"*De nada, gadjo*. Men must make compromises—it is wartime."

With a twinge of guilt, Tremaine protested. "No—no, you misunderstand; I married her willingly. Mora's been very good to me, and I can't complain." He paused to add with a trace of amusement, "So has the dog, actually."

He could see an answering gleam of amusement in the other man's eyes. "This is a great surprise to me."

"Yes. Well—I can't discuss private matters, but she—and the dog too, believe it or not—have been working to—to force me onto a better path, I guess you'd say." He paused, and then added honestly, "I was in bad shape, when we met."

The gypsy chief nodded. "I was a drunkard, once."

A bit taken aback, Tremaine was reminded that the gypsies tended to stay very well-informed; indeed, keeping abreast of information—especially local information—was how they managed to survive. After deciding he may as well be honest, he admitted, "My wife is a hard proctor, but that's exactly what I need. She won't give me the chance to have a relapse."

"It is a battle, every day," the other man replied. "I wish you luck."

He said nothing more, and Tremaine did not try to probe any further, since they seemed to have established a strange sort of affinity, and he didn't want to jeopardize it. They settled on a likely horse, and the *Baro* was willing to do an even trade—despite the fact it seemed clear to Tremaine that he'd got the better end of the deal.

When they walked back to the campfire, Tremaine saw that Mora had been gifted a colorful wrap by the other woman—with Mora's having immediately arranged the wrap around her shoulders, even though Tremaine knew the vibrant colors were not to her taste. "Is it not pretty?" she asked Tremaine.

"Very," he agreed, and thought—good; olive branches are being offered all around. It seems that everyone else has taken a cue from their *Baro*, who's allowed the *gadjo* to get the better of him in a horse trade.

In this notably lighter atmosphere, Tremaine transferred his saddle to his new mount, and the *Baro* asked, "When does Gerard return to camp? We will be moving on, soon." He paused, and then added, "I hear the *Afrancesados* are beating their swords."

Tremaine made no comment on the matter, since the Romanies may be well-informed but they didn't yet know that Señor Sanchez was in no shape to beat anything, anymore. Instead, he assured the gypsy chief, "I wouldn't think we'll keep Gerard more than a week, or so."

"*Bueno*. If you would, do not mention his name to anyone. The *Afrancesados* would be very much surprised to hear that he yet lives, and they must not be agitated more than they already are."

"Don't worry—I won't say anything; I have my own reasons."

Tremaine watched Gerard bid goodbye to his tribe, and thought—now, that's all very interesting; I think the *Baro* is trying to give me a warning, but I don't know how much he knows, and he doesn't know how much I know, and so neither one of us can speak freely. It would pay, perhaps, to get a better handle on the local *Afrancesados*, and find out what they're up to.

CHAPTER 24

They began the journey back to Cadiz, Tremaine and Mora walking abreast on the path along the river, whilst Gerard trailed behind—it seemed clear he was unhappy about his role in these events. As the horses stepped along, Tremaine decided to remark to Mora, "I hear you had a little run-in, with this group of gypsies."

"Gypsies will cheat you, if they have the chance," she replied, unfazed. "I do not like to be cheated."

"Well, I'm glad we left on friendlier terms; the gypsies tend to hear things, and some of the tribes were very helpful to the allies, during the war."

"This does not matter to me," she reminded him. "What matters to me is whether I am cheated."

"I will concede your point," he offered diplomatically, "but sometimes you have to overlook an ally's shortcomings. The gypsies are useful because they tend to keep abreast of what is happening in any given area—they have to, in order to survive—and it is important for an army to have an ear to the ground, so to speak."

"I would not wish to rely on a gypsy's tale," she observed, unmoved. "They lie like they breathe."

"A fair point, in some cases," he agreed. "And that's why the task of information-gathering is so difficult; we had to compare what we were being told with what is known. Trying to figure out whose information should be trusted is always a priority—and is always changing, sometimes from one day to the next."

She glanced at him, dubious. "Such a thing seems foolish. It is far better to trust no one."

Tremaine realized that perhaps his wife was not the sort of person who was inclined to understand the importance of espionage, and so he only offered, "Perhaps not, but nonetheless, it's important to try to find out what the enemy is planning."

"Why is this?"

The question seemed genuine, and—rather surprised by it—he explained, "So that you can make counterplans."

She continued skeptical, and knit her brow. "Wouldn't you fight them, just the same?"

He thought about it. "Well, yes—you have to be strong, but strategy is important, too. A great deal of war's success is having up-to-date information—and giving out false information, too."

She tilted her head in mild disagreement. "You can only win if you are stronger. In the end, nothing else matters."

"Yes, but I suppose that's where the gathering of information comes in—to help make the enemy weaker. A good example is what the Englishman did, when he asked you to sabotage Napoleon's supplies; if an army has no weapons or food, it is made much weaker."

She considered this, and nodded fairly. "*Si;* this is true."

Since she'd made a concession, he thought he'd make one of his own. "Your men are rather like the *guerrillas,* in that way—a small, determined force can wreak havoc on a much larger one. Those of us who fight traditional warfare have no idea how to counter being repeatedly punched in the face by such an irregular army—Napoleon included."

Pleased, she smiled slightly. "*Si.*"

"And speaking of such, I'm amazed that the *guerrillas* never nosed-out your operation on the mountain. They're a bit like the gypsies—they tend to know everything, and these southern mountains are their home turf."

"I would not like to fight the *guerrillas*," she admitted.

With a rueful smile, he acknowledged, "I think the Englishman would agree with you."

She glanced at him. "He is not so clever, perhaps, if they have bested him."

But Tremaine only shrugged. "The Englishman has one aim—rather like you do—only instead of saving slaves, his aim is to save his country from Napoleon. He has to work with whatever allies he can to achieve that aim, and he doesn't appreciate it when he's not kept informed, or when his supposed allies are working at cross-purposes. You can hardly blame him, Mora."

With a shrug, she returned to her original premise. "It is better to trust no one; then there is no 'cross-purposes'."

"Without the allies, though, it is impossible to be the stronger," he countered.

She turned to him with a small smile. "We speak of the same thing, Robert; I do not say there is no need for allies, I am saying you would be foolish to trust them not to do what is in their own interests."

Since this seemed a fair point—and one the British had learned the hard way, many a time—he decided to change the subject. "The *Baro* asked that we be careful not to reveal Gerard's identity; apparently the *Afrancesados* think he is dead, and he would be valuable to them."

"*Si*—he could bring down much trouble for us. I do not want him—it is the Englishman, who said he must come."

But Tremaine felt compelled to point out, "The Englishman's got the right of it, though; we need to make certain the mining operation will be worth the trouble. Sometimes what looks like gold isn't, and Gerard can tell the difference. There's a lot of hard work to be done, and you'll want to be certain from the start that it will be worth it."

She sighed. "Then we must tolerate the gypsy, and hope that he does not cheat us. If he does, he will pay."

He smiled at her attitude—which only served to demonstrate what they'd just discussed; her people were not inclined to cobble together a fragile coalition via diplomacy and soothing words—in her world, only might made right. Which was in direct contrast to the slow-goings at the Congress of Vienna —maybe if the diplomats were forced to fight each other hand-to-hand in order to achieve their goals, some immediate progress could be made.

They continued to walk along—they were in no hurry, since they planned to spend another day in Cadiz—and Tremaine offered, "I'll bet when you were harrying the ships in Cadiz, you never thought that you'd wind-up married to a Welshman and running a mine in Spain."

"I do not think about what is to come," she replied. "And so, it does not surprise me."

"I wish I could do the same," he confessed. "It certainly makes life easier to bear."

But she shook her head. "There is no 'bearing,' Robert; I am going to help you dig your gold, and whenever I need to rest, I will lay by the stream. I will watch the clouds go over the mountain, and I will think of nothing."

Amused by the picture thus presented, he teased, "May I lie beside you?"

"You think too much," she pointed out.

"I will try very hard to think of nothing," he offered.

Graciously, she agreed. "Very well—you may lie beside me."

"Will we have children?" He was curious, because the subject hadn't yet arisen; strange, to think that he and this untamed desert-dweller would have mutual children—but the idea didn't seem half so far-fetched as it would have a week ago.

She nodded. "I would like this. Beautiful little girls, who are happy and free."

He smiled. "Like you."

But her answer surprised him. "No, Robert. I will never be happy, and I will never be free. It is why we are the same."

A bit shocked, he made no reply and they made the rest of the journey back to Cadiz in silence.

CHAPTER 25

When they returned to San Ysidro, the banker wasn't at his usual chair on his store-front porch, but instead his place had been taken by a younger man—rather sleek-looking, and dressed in an immaculate suit.

"Ho," Tremaine called-out in a friendly fashion, as he pulled up for a moment. "Are you new here? I'll be happy when someone else is newer than me."

The young man chuckled. "I am Señor Ruiz's new clerk. My name is Diego de la Vega."

"I am pleased to meet you, Señor. I am Robert Tremaine, and this is Señora Tremaine. We bring with us Señor Gomez, who we have hired to help with our sheep."

"I am happy to meet you," the young man said. "You return from Gibraltar?"

"Cadiz," Tremaine replied easily. "I mean no disrespect to Señor Sanchez, but I needed to find a better horse." With a gesture, he indicated his new mount.

"Ah—I wondered if perhaps you'd traveled there with him."

Tremaine feigned surprise. "Is Señor Sanchez away, also?"

The young man shrugged, but his causal manner was at odds with the sharpness of his gaze, as it rested on them. "*Si.* It is a little strange—his shop is closed, and no one knows where he has gone."

"Did he owe you money?" Tremaine joked. "We must hunt him down."

Immediately, the man disclaimed in a light-hearted fashion. "No, no—I am certain he will return soon."

They declined the clerk's offer of refreshment, and continued onward to the path up the mountain. With the gypsy chief's oblique warning in mind, Tremaine said to Mora in a low voice, "This Diego fellow seems a bit unsettled by Sanchez's disappearance. Is he in the *Afrancesado* network—do you know of him?"

She chided gently, "You must not speak of these things, Robert."

"Fair enough—but this may be important; I don't like the looks of him—unless it was the

Englishman who placed him there, of course." He glanced at her.

"The Englishman does not speak of these things, either." This, said with the slightest hint of rebuke, because he wasn't complying with her warning.

But Tremaine persisted, trying to put his feeling into words. "This relates back to what I spoke of—how important it is to watch, and gather information. I had the sense that the gypsy chief was giving me a warning about recent *Afrancesado* movements, and now suddenly we have Diego, who seems a bit too—a bit too sophisticated, for this outpost. He doesn't strike me as a banker's clerk."

"I don't think anyone truly wishes to be a banker's clerk," she replied in a dry tone.

"Probably true. What happened to the last one?"

She shrugged. "One morning—about a month ago—he is gone. He took much of the bank's money with him."

But Tremaine found this all rather ominous, and persisted, "Does anyone know this for certain?"

She raised her brows. "You are suspicious?"

"Yes," he replied bluntly. "This Diego fellow's not right."

After a moment's pause, Mora informed him, "The banker, Señor Ruiz, belongs to the Englishman."

Blowing out a relieved breath, Tremaine told her

with all sincerity, "Thank you for telling me—I would have worried about it."

"*De nada*," she said with a small smile. "You must not be made to worry."

As they continued on their journey up the mountain, Tremaine decided that he'd make a few inquiries on the quiet, anyway. He had to keep in mind that Mora didn't have the experience he had, in weighing people and their motives—her methods were far more straightforward. And despite the banker's allegiance to the British, it was certainly possible that his clerk was a secret *Afrancesado;* his old commander might be keeping an eye on things here, but he couldn't be expected to know everything. Not to mention there was the gypsy's warning—although the warning itself may not have been sincere, but instead an attempt to sow suspicion amongst allies. As Mora had correctly pointed out, it was probably best to trust no one; the war had made for some unexpected alliances, but these alliances would be fragile, since each of the players would always pursue their own interests first. Trust was something in short order, nowadays, with everyone scrambling to prepare for the next war.

And with this in mind, it didn't seem a coincidence that the last bank clerk had suddenly disappeared—along with a sum of money—and that this one seemed an unlikely sort of replacement. Sleek, sophisticated Diego, who sat on the porch watching the comings and goings, and who'd thought they would know what had happened to Sanchez.

Suddenly struck, Tremaine wondered for a moment if the Spanish *guerrillas* had taken-out the last clerk. and then planted this Diego fellow in his place so as to—in turn—keep an eye on the banker who'd been put into place by the British. After all, it did seem strange that the *guerrillas* hadn't taken a more active interest in what was happening up at the mountain pass—this Andalusian mountain region was their home base.

Almost immediately, however, he decided this was unlikely; Diego was far too soft to be working for the *guerrillas*. And in any event, the *guerrillas* weren't shy creatures; if they'd caught wind of the British siphoning operation at the homestead, they probably wouldn't have hesitated to step in and do a bit of siphoning, themselves. Lord, it was just as well that they hadn't caught wind—one could only imagine the scorched earth, if it came to a war between the Moroccan pirates and the Spanish *guerrillas*.

So, maybe he was jumping at shadows—and in any event, he'd forgot a major point; if Diego had been placed into his current position by the *Afrancesados*, surely Mora would have been made aware of it, since the *Afrancesados* believed that she was allied with them.

Unless—unless the *Afrancesados* had somehow become aware that Mora was not what she seemed, and that she'd been double-crossing them, all along.

This thought was alarming, and gave him pause. If they discovered that Mora had been killing their men, sabotaging their supplies, and stealing their money, they wouldn't hesitate to go scorched-earth, themselves. He'd best find out whether she'd been exposed, and soon; he still had that instinct—despite having done his best to dull it with drink—and that instinct was sending out alarms. Something wasn't right about Diego, and how he'd replaced the former bank clerk.

With these troubling thoughts foremost in his mind, he said little for the remainder of the journey and wished—oh, how he wished—that he still had his flask, to help put his mind at rest.

CHAPTER 26

They'd been back at the homestead for two days, and—after a rudimentary sluice-box had been constructed—the workers were now engaged in the hard work of damming up the stream, so as to direct the faster-flowing water through the sluice-box.

The Moroccan men worked without complaint, and seemed to have forgiven Tremaine for having hoodwinked them—indeed, it only appeared to have improved his standing, in their eyes.

Nonetheless, they were obviously keeping a sharp eye out, because that morning they'd grabbed their guns and alerted Mora, even before Tremaine himself had noticed the silhouette of a rider, watching their work from the crest of the pass.

Mora said something in their own language to her

men, and then explained to Tremaine, "It is the British. The Englishman said he will send two men."

Tremaine shielded his eyes with his hand, carefully scouring the ridge. "I only see the one."

"The other one approaches around from the other side of the peak—I had to lock Sahim in the house, he was so eager to give chase. But it would hurt the Englishman's feelings to find out that I knew his man approached, and so I pretend not to know he is there."

A bit defensively, Tremaine said, "You can hardly blame him for being cautious."

"No," she agreed. "But I am just as careful as he."

After the two British men introduced themselves, they were also put to work at the dam site. They'd know soon enough what they had; they needed only a sampling of the heavier minerals that would be caught in the sluice to allow Gerard to decide if the game was worth the candle, so to speak. Oftentimes, felspar or pyrite could fool even the savviest miner, which is why it was important to have an experienced assayer do some testing at the onset.

As for the Romany man, Gerard seemed content to watch the others do the work whilst he spent a great deal of time meandering barefoot in the stream, idly scrutinizing the streambed. Occasionally, he'd reach down to lift a sampling of the coarse pebbles, running them through his fingers so that they dropped back into the water again, and Tremaine was left with the distinct impression that the man was pretending to do something useful so that he wouldn't be asked to join in the hard labor.

"What do you think?" Tremaine had asked him, since it was impossible to gauge his thoughts.

"It is promising," the gypsy had agreed, almost grudgingly. "I see salt minerals in in the stream, also. If I could have a sack, I will collect samples."

"Our focus is gold, though—it's the more valuable," Tremaine explained, hiding his impatience with the man for not grasping this obvious fact. "Anything else will have to take second priority. Ask Mora for an old grain sack, if you wish—she'll have some."

When Gerard returned to the stream with his sack, Mora also emerged from the homestead, coming over to offer honey-loaves to the workers.

Tremaine took the welcome opportunity to lean against his shovel for a moment, and as Mora gave him his honey-cake, she asked in a low voice, "What does the gypsy do?"

"He's looking to test samples of the rocks from the streambed for other elements, and I suppose there's no harm in it. Only the heaviest minerals will be harvested by the sluice-box, so he'll test to see if there's anything else of interest in the stream bed. It will keep him busy—there's not much for him to do until we can come up with a sufficient sampling of gold."

Her eyes slid to his. "He could work, alongside the others."

But Tremaine only shrugged. "His value is not in his muscles, Mora. And anyway, I know his type; he'd only complain and cause trouble, if we put him to work."

They stood for a few moments, watching the others. "You must not tell the gypsy about the stockpile," she warned.

Amused, he eyed her. "You think he wanted a sack because he's going to rob us, and steal away in the night?"

"He is a gypsy," she replied, as though this was all the explanation that was needed.

Since she'd brought up the subject, he decided to ask, "I wouldn't know how to tell him about the stockpile in the first place. Is it well-hidden?"

Readily, she disclosed, "There is an iron lockbox, buried beneath the hay crib in the barn."

He nodded. "Is there a key?"

"No," she said. You brush the straw away, and you will see a ring to pull."

He glanced at the other men, who sat beside the stream, eating in silence—not much fraternizing, between these two groups. "Do your men know about it?"

Amused, she replied, "They are the ones who buried the box, Robert."

But he only defended, "I suppose I've taken your lesson to heart, about not trusting anyone, just now."

She shrugged. If my men wish to kill us, they will kill us."

He had to chuckle. "That doesn't exactly reassure me."

She unbent enough to explain, "They are content to reap the profits—they have sent much money to their families. And they know if they try to come against me, they will be made to pay."

He glossed over the unfortunate fact that there was little chance that any sort of justice would be meted-out, if this motley group decided to abscond with the stockpile, and instead asked, "How do you go about transferring the stockpile over to the British?"

Patiently, she explained, "The stockpile is not for the British, Robert."

This was something of a surprise, but—on second thought—it did make sense; after all, his spymaster would want what was due to him from this enterprise as soon as possible, and there would be no point to burying it in the barn. On the other hand, it was interesting that she didn't send every penny of her own portion over to the Knights' operation in Algiers. Perhaps she needed to keep a fair amount of money and weapons close at hand; after all, these were uncertain times, and if push came to shove, they'd have to be certain they could bribe or fight their way onto a ship bound for Morocco.

So; hopefully she wasn't withholding money that was actually due to the British, since that would put him in a cleft stick—best not even try to find out. He'd his own competing factions to placate—between his new bride and the British army—and God forbid he'd ever have to choose between them.

With this in mind, he tentatively suggested, "The barn may not be the best place to hide such a stockpile, Mora."

But she only shrugged. "I do not trust the banker in town—he belongs to the Englishman."

"Very well," he readily agreed, hoping she didn't see in his suggestion an attempt to cheat her—there seemed to be a theme that such an attempt tended to be dangerous to one's health. And since they were discussing these matters, it seemed a good time to raise his excuse for doing some fact-finding in town. "I should ride down to San Ysidro tomorrow, if that's agreeable. Now that I think of it, I should have obtained another copy of our marriage lines to send along to the Colonel at the British garrison. If I am killed, the Spanish government could raise a dispute about who owns the land, but it's unlikely they'll want to lock horns with the British army."

"How long?" she asked.

"It shouldn't take more than a day. By then, the dam should be complete and we can attempt the first run with the sluice-box."

She was silent for a moment, and then she lifted her unreadable gaze to his. "You will not drink. I will have your promise, as an English gentleman."

Surprised, he readily agreed. "No—I promise." In fact, is was rather interesting that this hadn't even occurred to him; in the past, he'd have gone to great lengths to plot-out an opportunity to have a private hour with the bottle, with none the wiser.

"And you must not think too much," she warned.

"*Si*, Señora," he agreed in a meek tone. "I will try to think as little as I possibly can."

CHAPTER 27

And so, the following afternoon found Tremaine tying up his horse at the town's church, and climbing the wooden stairs to knock on the door. He'd learned long ago—back when he was trusted to do reconnaissance—that the best way to get information about the goings-on in a local area was to beguile the town gossip.

Señora Frasco answered the door, and immediately brightened upon seeing him. "Señor Tremaine—how good to see you. The Padre is still at the reception, but he should return soon."

As she took his hat and coat, Tremaine asked in a friendly fashion, "Someone got married?"

The woman made a sympathetic sound. "No—a funeral, instead. Señor Ruiz—a very sad day."

Tremaine stilled for a moment. "The banker?"

"*Si*—we must hope Diego can handle his business until another banker is sent from Madrid." With a look, she indicated to him that she was not at all certain that this was the case.

In the polite tones of someone who is not personally affected either way, he replied, "Well, that's a shame; I did not realize Señor Ruiz was ill, poor man."

As she escorted him into the parlor, the woman was quick to explain, "No—no; he was kicked by his horse. A blow to the head, and he was done." Sadly, she shook her head. "The Padre said it only goes to show—you do not know the time, nor the hour."

Tremaine made a show of courteous, casual condolence. "I'm sorry for it—didn't know him at all, of course. And I hate to be a pest at such a time, but I was hoping you'd be willing to draw up another copy of my marriage lines." A bit sheepishly, he added, "My family in Wales keeps a Bible with all the records, and I should do my part."

"Of course, of course," she assured him, barely hiding her glee at this unlooked-for opportunity to have a tête-a-tête with a presentable man. "It is no trouble—no trouble at all; come, sit down and I will bring the tea cakes I saved from the reception."

"Thank you; I am sorry to plague you on such a day."

Fussing, she indicated that he should take a seat

at the parlor table, which was covered with a hand-crocheted little cloth that was no doubt the work of her own hands. "Not at all, not at all. Shall I light another candle? It is turning dark. Will you take wine? I have a bottle of the local sherry—we must console ourselves, after such a tragedy."

"Of course," he said immediately, since he'd the shrewd suspicion that she'd been making inroads into the sherry well before his arrival—which was a stroke of luck; no better way to elicit information than by conducting a flirtation with a tipsy older woman. He'd be careful, though—he'd promised Mora, and so he'd have to find a way to pretend he was imbibing more than he was.

She retrieved her copy of his marriage lines, and then brought her writing materials to the table—showing no inclination to hurry, as she poured the sherry and deposited the plate of tea-cakes. When she finally settled into her chair, she met his gaze in innocent inquiry. "You did not bring your wife, today?"

"No," he replied, in the carefully neutral tones of a man who is not eager to discuss his wife. "She stayed behind—there were a few projects, requiring her attention."

"Of course, of course." Señora Frasco began copying-out the document, and slid her gaze to his with an arch expression. "Your family will be surprised by your choice, perhaps."

He chuckled, since the best way to lay the groundwork for confidences was to give up some of your own—whether truthful or not. Nevertheless, he had to be careful not to openly criticize Mora, since such a thing would be out-of-keeping for the façade that he was presenting. "They will, won't they? But it will have to wait; I have no plans to take her home to meet them, at present."

She raised her brows, as she scratched-out a few more words. "Oh? You plan to stay the winter on the mountain?"

"It's just as cold, in Wales," he joked a bit ruefully. "And besides, I can't leave my sheep."

"Ah, yes; you will raise sheep. You have hired some help, now."

So—she must have heard about the encounter with Diego, as they'd come back to town. Not a surprise; in a small town, newcomers were always an item of intense interest.

"*Si*; Gomez will help me with the shearing, when it comes time."

"And your wife, she will help, also?" This, said with a slight touch of incredulity.

He chuckled, subtly joining-in with the woman's implied criticism. "Believe it or not, she used to raise sheep, growing-up."

His companion paused to stare at him. "This is so?"

"It is," he agreed, and topped off their glasses; he needed to steer the conversation into more fruitful areas, and to this end it seemed that more wine was needed. "My wife is a very interesting woman."

The señora glanced at him from under her lashes, with a look that could pass for coyness in a younger woman. "*Si*—she is very interesting, indeed. How do you find married life, Señor Tremaine?"

He shrugged, with a show of polite respect. "I can't complain; I gained the land, and Mora gained a husband."

She arched her brows, as she sprinkled the sand over the wet ink. "Yes—we were all very surprised to hear that Tosada had deeded her the land."

It seems that she's very well-informed, he thought with a twinge of caution; but it's not as though it was a secret—Sanchez knew about the deed, certainly. Suddenly reminded, he wondered if the deed to the homestead was still secure, now that the banker was dead. I should have had a copy made, he realized—although now that the British are aware of the situation, it's not as important—the garrison will back me up, if a dispute arises.

Bringing his focus back to the task at hand, he shrugged with all the appearance of a man who was reluctant to criticize his wife. "It was my good fortune, though. I gained a strong wife and a fine plot of land, all at once."

"*Si, si,*" she agreed, taking her cue to change the subject from Mora. "You are a fortunate man."

Taking this opportunity to steer the conversation toward his object, he remarked, "Not like Señor Ruiz, poor fellow. If I was superstitious, I would be afraid to cross the bank's threshold; I understand the last clerk absconded with the funds."

Leaning back, his companion negligently held her glass aloft as she made a derisive sound. "A scoundrel, that one. Our last priest was a scoundrel, too—he was a drunkard, and *doy gracias al Señor* they replaced him with the Padre." She then took a rather defiant swallow.

An alarm went off in Tremaine's head, and he took his own swallow of sherry so as to allow for a pause before he casually asked the next question. "You like this new priest better?"

"Oh—*si, si,*" she agreed, in the owlish tones of an older woman who'd drunk a bit too much. She nodded wisely. "This one—this one is much better."

"How long has he been here?"

She squinted, thinking about it. "Almost a month."

So; the circuit priest had been replaced around the same time that the former bank clerk had disappeared, and there was a pattern developing that he couldn't quite like. The important thing was to keep this woman talking, and so he refilled their glasses and inquired, "Perhaps the Padre knows Diego—and that is how he managed to get the clerking position at the bank. It would make sense—I think they are both from Madrid."

But the woman shook her head, pleased to have superior information. "No—no; Diego is from Aranjuez, instead." She leaned in and lowered her voice, even though it was only the two of them in the house. "Diego is connected to the old king."

"Charles?" Tremaine asked in surprise. The former Spanish king had been in exile—ever since Napoleon had put his own brother on the Spanish throne. But now, with Napoleon's brother ousted, the current king was Ferdinand, Charles's despised son.

Frowning, he contemplated the table-top, trying to process this information—he was having a bit of trouble concentrating, but this was important; if Diego was a Spanish royalist, then mayhap his suspicion—that he was somehow involved with the *Afrancesados*—was unfounded. In fact, it was entirely possible that the sleek aristocrat had wound-up in this backwater town because he'd ruffled the wrong feathers—the old Spanish aristocrats were famous for their feuds, and for suffering insult from the merest slight.

Which meant that—perhaps—he'd got it wrong,

and there was nothing suspicious about the old clerk's disappearance, the new priest's appearance, and how Diego seemed ill-suited for his current position. After all, he'd been wrong before—which was why it was always wise to follow-up, and not operate on a hunch. Save that there was something else—something else, here, that he was forgetting; something important—

Aloud, he mused, "I was—that's something of a surprise; I was a bit worried that he was an *Afrancesado*. There was—there was a ring of them, operating here during the war."

"*Madre de Dios*—no, no," his companion assured him with a chuckle, as she poured more sherry. "Instead, he is loyal to the old king."

Suddenly struck, Tremaine frowned. "But—but isn't the old court still in exile? How did Diego manage to make his way here?"

For an instant, a wary expression flashed across the woman's face—so quickly that another may not have noticed. Then she shrugged, and chuckled again, as she gave him a knowing look. "Do not repeat it, but I think there was woman-trouble—Diego is just the sort to drink from another's cistern. The old king has sent him off, so that he can cause no more mischief."

But Tremaine had recognized that flash of wariness in her eyes, and felt his stomach drop as he remembered the thing he'd forgot; the spymaster's liaison—the banker—was suddenly dead, and under suspicious circumstances.

With a massive effort, he nodded benignly as he fingered the stem of his glass with his gaze downcast. Lord almighty, but he was an idiot, to be making assumptions without knowing the lay of the land. He'd been hoping to get this woman talking and now—now he'd the unhappy sense that it was he, who'd been doing the talking.

With a small smile, he met her gaze with his own teasing one. "Say no more; some things never change." With a reluctant sigh, he put his hands on the table and steadied himself as he rose. "And speaking of such, I must find my bed at the inn."

"So soon? The Padre should return at any time—a few minutes more, I will open another bottle."

"No—but thank you; the sherry was excellent, as was the company." Carefully, he folded the parchment and secured it in his waistcoat. "I'll send the copy to my family—it will be something of a shock—I'm sure they never thought I'd marry."

The Señora tittered in a tipsy way. "No more a shock than for us, here in town; an Englishman, of all things; come to marry the Mademoiselle."

Hiding his abject dismay, he gave no indication that the woman had just given her role away and instead, bowed to her a bit unsteadily. "*Muchas gracias* for the hospitality—and for your charming company."

"With a coquettish look—or at least, the echo of a coquettish look from her youth—she offered, "Perhaps I could accompany you, back to your room."

With a gallant gesture, he took her hand and kissed the back. "Thank you, *bella Señora*, but I value my life too much."

She laughed, but he could see the calculation in her eyes—she wasn't sure whether he was as stupid as he seemed.

But he was indeed stupid, and—castigating himself—he offered-up one last, lingering smile as he made his way through the door, fighting the urge to run.

CHAPTER 28

It was growing dark, as Tremaine began his hurried ascent up the mountain, feeling ten times a fool and cursing himself for being a dupe. Whatever the situation was—and he was a bit too fuddled to grasp it, just now—he'd the certain conviction that he needed to warn Mora immediately, and extract her from the homestead with all speed.

Urging his horse to step lively—lucky he was good quality—he was almost relieved when Sahim appeared on the trail, wagging his tail in greeting and then falling-in alongside to trot beside the horse. In a strange way, the dog's presence was reassuring; he'd been a bit panicked—thinking that the situation was urgent—but obviously, if the *Afrancesados* were suspicious of Mora's true allegiances, they would have to move very carefully, since caution was advised when it came to her and her men. He need only confess to his blundering, and get her out as quickly and quietly as possible—no need to panic.

When he finally saw the light from the homestead, he was equal parts relieved and apprehensive; the colder night air had helped clear his head a bit, but Mora would know he'd been drinking—she'd know that he'd broken his promise.

He slid off his horse as she appeared, silhouetted in the doorway and holding a lantern aloft. "Robert," she said. "I will help you with your horse."

He stood for a moment, leaning against the horse to stay steady and trying to think of what he should say. "I'm so sorry," was what he came up with.

But she only took the horse's reins from him, and grasped his elbow to steer him toward the barn. "Tell me what has happened."

He bent his head, relieved beyond measure that she knew that he wouldn't have broken his word without good cause. "I think I've stepped in it, Mora. I had a drink or two with Señora Frasco—tried to get her talking—and I—I spoke of things I shouldn't have. I'm worried she's an *Afrancesado*—she—she slipped, and called you the Mademoiselle. She was—she was wondering why you'd married an Englishman."

She nodded, and threw-up a stirrup to begin unbuckling the saddle's girth until he moved into place to take the task from her. She asked, "Did she speak of Gerard?"

He blinked, and for the first time noticed that all the other horses were missing from the barn. "Gerard is an *Afrancesado*? Good God; what's happened?"

With a deft movement, Mora reached to pull the horse's bridle over his head. "Gerard took a horse and stole away this morning, just after you left. The other men were working, and did not notice for many hours." In a dispassionate voice, she added, "The Englishman was a fool, to trust a gypsy."

But Tremaine was frowning, as he considered this unwelcome news. "No—the Englishman's no fool, Mora. There's no way he'd jeopardize this chance to set-up a working gold mine."

"If you say," she replied with little conviction, and turned to hang the bridle on the peg.

He glanced around the barn—empty, save for the chickens and the sheep. "Where are the other men?"

"My men went to find Gerard. He cannot be trusted, and we cannot allow word of the gold to spread. When the British men learned of this, they went after my men to stop them from killing Gerard."

Tremaine ran a hand over his head. "I know it looks bad, but Gerard's a valuable asset—you can't just kill him. The Englishman—"

"I do not obey the Englishman," she reminded

him abruptly. Taking his arm, she said, "Come; we will discuss what must be done."

"We've got to clear out," he said immediately, as she steered him toward the main building. "That's what I was coming to tell you—I've got a bad feeling." Trying desperately to sort-out his thoughts, he informed her, "The banker—Señor Ruiz—is dead."

She glanced up at him, as she maneuvered him through the door. "This is so?"

"Yes—Señora Frasco said he'd been kicked by a horse, but it's all too smoky. And I found out that the priest was replaced at the same time the last bank clerk disappeared; it's too—it's too much a coincidence, for a little place like this. And so—and so I pressed a bit, and the woman told me that Diego is connected to the old king—King Charles—but when I wondered how he came to be here, since the old court is still in exile—I could see that she was unhappy she'd been tripped up."

"This is good information, Robert," she said with approval, as she guided him into the bedroom. "But you must not drink, anymore."

"I broke my promise. I'm so sorry, Mora."

Putting pressure on his shoulders so that he sat down on the bed, she gave him her grave smile. "But rather than run to tell your news to the Englishman, you came to warn me. It is much appreciated."

"You're my wife," he replied, surprised that she

was surprised. "And you're in grave danger, if they suspect you've been double-dealing and killing their men. We've got to clear out." Blowing out a breath, he added. "It's a damned shame, that all this has to happen just as the men are away, chasing Gerard."

She said nothing, but he read her aright, and was forced to add a bit heavily, "Which seems to indicate that Gerard's thrown-in with the *Afrancesados*."

"The Englishman was a fool, to trust a gypsy," she pronounced again.

He met her eyes, as she helped him slide his coat off. "It looks as though they're setting-up an attack. We've got to clear out, Mora—clear out at first light."

In a practical tone, she replied, "We will take weapons and ammunition, and go to the cave in the morning. And then, we will wait to see what happens."

Stubbornly he countered, "We will double-up on my horse, and escape through the pass. We need to clear out."

"I will not leave my men to be ambushed," she replied steadily.

There was a small pause. "Of course," he acknowledged, gripping her arm briefly in a gesture of apology. "I forgot." He thought about it for a moment. "We can lay a false trail over the pass, and with any luck, the enemy will give chase. Then we can intercept the other men before they return—warn them that everyone needs to clear out."

She shook her head slightly, as she knelt to address his boots. "No; we stay here."

He stared at the top of her head. "If they've uncovered your role, they will be out for blood."

"Everyone is always out for blood, Robert. I do not leave the gold."

He was silent, because even in his fuddled state he was reminded that this only to be expected—she didn't much care who was out to get her; her answer to every challenge was to fight, and fight hard. Because the on-going plots and counter-plots between the factions from the last war didn't matter in the least to her; she only cared about her own operation—funding the Knights in Algiers—and if she sparked off a war in the mountains of Spain, it hardly mattered. She came from a land of tribal warlords, and she would give as good as she got.

It was an alien perspective for someone like him, who viewed war as a series of clandestine operations—where chess pieces were constantly being moved about, and the last needful thing was to take a bold stand, and let the chips fall where they may. In a strange way, he found himself suddenly envious of her—of her unshakable dedication. She threw no recriminations his way—even though he well-deserved them—but instead, looked to fight the next fight without a moment's regret or second-guessing. Other people might think she was cold to the core, but he knew better; instead, she was single-mindedly focused on achieving her goal—siphoning funds from anyone who still had them. Which, in turn, meant that she was going-up against some of the most powerful operatives in the world and convincing them—either by force or by wile—to cooperate with her. It was extraordinary, but it was also a testament to that single-minded focus, born of her own misery.

And it was a testament to the spymaster that he'd seen in Mora a possible solution to the problem that was Robert Tremaine, formerly of his Majesty's diplomatic service. If she couldn't fix him, no one could.

But unfortunately, the spymaster's plan had set off the chain of events which had brought them to their current situation; the remnants of the *Afrancesados* in this area—already quietly preparing for Napoleon's return—had started taking a hard look at why the notorious Mademoiselle would be willing to marry a former English officer, and then take him up to live with her at their waystation. And he'd made matters worse by falling into a trap like a green recruit; he'd thought to wean some information from the town gossip, and instead, an *Afrancesado* spy had easily weaned information from him.

I've let everyone down again, he realized with a sting of shame. As Mora would say, I spoke of things that shouldn't be spoken of, and now we're both in grave danger, as a result.

In a fit of remorse, he grasped her hand to stay it, as she pulled off a boot. "I've mucked things up, Mora; I'm worse than all your other husbands combined."

She leaned back on her haunches and looked up at him, the light from the lantern flickering across her face. "I will tell you a secret, Robert; I was never married. I only said this so you would not think I was a *puta*—you are a British gentleman, and you would not marry me if you thought this."

He assured her, "I don't think you are a *puta*, and I wouldn't care if you were. You're extraordinary, and I wish I'd half your mettle."

"I make you harder, and you make me softer," she reminded him, as she rose to blow out the lantern's candle. "It is a good bargain, I think. Now sleep; we rise early tomorrow."

CHAPTER 29

In the pre-dawn darkness, they were readying to retreat to the caves, but as Tremaine hoisted a sack of musket-balls to tie to his horse, a new problem suddenly presented itself. "What shall we do with the horse? If we lay a false trail over the pass, we can't very well leave him in the meadow."

"We can take him to the caves, and shoot him," she suggested.

He winced, even as he knew she was only being practical, but he was reminded of the British army's retreat at Portugal, when the officers had to shoot their own horses so that the enemy would not gain them—another horrific memory he tried not to think about. "We'll take him into the caves and hide him, instead. We'll need him, regardless of what happens."

"He is a gypsy horse," she replied skeptically. "He deserves to be shot."

"I'll override you on this, Mora," he said firmly. "We'll use him to carry the ammunition to the caves, and then I'll lay a false trail over the pass and circle around over the crags. That way, his footprints coming back won't be obvious."

"Very well," she said, although he knew she remained skeptical.

"Let's go; I think it's light enough to see."

With silent determination, they led the laden horse across the meadow toward the caves, the long meadow grass a bit frosty at this early hour. Sahim trotted along beside them until suddenly he stopped, his slim head raised. Mora stopped also, watching the dog.

"Keep going," Tremaine urged in a quiet tone. "The sun's coming up."

The dog growled, low in his throat, and immediately Mora yanked on Tremaine's arm. "Down," she urged.

Two things happened almost simultaneously; the sound of a musket shot echoed from just ahead of them, and the horse grunted, collapsing to the ground.

The flash of gunfire gave Tremaine the location of

the attacker, and he immediately ran forward at full speed—if there were others, which was likely, any return gunfire would betray their position. Running hard as he drew his knife, he made out the dim figure of a man just as the other was bringing-up his musket again—good; the man's hands were occupied and if Tremaine could close quickly, he'd be unable to defend himself.

But to his surprise, he was nearly knocked off his feet by Sahim, streaking past and launching himself upon the attacker, with the man going down heavily on his back.

Terrified screams were cut short, as the attacker's throat was torn out and Tremaine found he had to look away, reminded of the sheep he'd seen back home after the wolves had got to them.

There was no time to rest, though, as another shot rang out from just behind him, with the musket-ball whizzing past his ear—it was still too dark for the enemy to shoot accurately, but it was getting lighter by the minute. Meanwhile, Mora was pinned down, and she didn't dare shoot for fear of hitting him or the dog. Since there'd be a few seconds whilst this new attacker was reloading—muskets could only shoot one ball at a time—Tremaine crouched low and hoped the dog would obey him; "Sahim," he urged; "Go get 'em."

But no urging was necessary, as the animal had

already wheeled from his last victim to streak toward the next, and as the startled man screamed in gurgling horror, Tremaine took the opportunity to sprint toward the fallen horse.

He dove behind the carcass, where Mora already lay flat, resting her musket barrel on the dead animal. "How many?" he panted.

"There is at least one more, to the south," she replied, indicating the opposite direction from the other two. "But we have only the one musket."

Startled, he looked to see that his own weapon lay beneath the fallen horse—there would be no chance to retrieve it from under a thousand pounds of inert animal.

"I've my pistol," he said, as he drew it. "Fire when you will." This, because they'd need a second weapon ready to fire, or else the enemy would take advantage of the time it took for them to reload the musket.

Almost on cue, the sun appeared over the peak and began flooding the meadow with light. It was to their advantage; anyone approaching across the broad meadow would now be clearly visible, and indeed, two men could be seen suddenly crouching, as the advancing sunlight revealed their position.

Mora took careful aim and fired, but the ball missed—at this distance, accuracy was not to be expected—and the men took the opportunity to scramble back into the crags as Tremaine fired a shot after them for emphasis.

They waited in tense silence for a few minutes, with Tremaine almost startled to realize that Sahim was now lying behind them, having returned from his attack with barely a sound. The dog's teeth were still bloody, as he lay alert and panting on the grass, his ribs showing as his sides heaved in and out. He was an imposing weapon, this Arrow of Death, but he'd only be exposed on the meadow also, if he was sent to attack the other two. It was a mutual standoff, at present, but Tremaine knew that it wouldn't remain so.

"There're out of range, but we can't stay here," he said, as he reached to untie the ammo sack from the dead horse. "Now that we're pinned down, they'll split up, and one will circle around to surround us—and there may be more than just the two. We've got to get back into the homestead before they get into position."

"*Si*," she agreed.

"Get ready to run; I'll cover for you."

"No; you will run, and I will cover for you."

He couldn't help but smile, as he saw the futility of argument. "Right then; we'll both go together. Ready? On three. One, two—"

"Wait," she said. "I will send Sahim to draw their fire."

This was actually not a bad idea—if the dog drew enemy fire, it would give them some precious seconds to escape whilst the enemy was reloading. Nevertheless, he couldn't resist pointing out, "They won't hesitate to shoot him, Mora."

"I wish them luck," she replied, and spoke to the dog in her own language.

The dog lifted its ears and gazed at her.

With a bit more urgency, Mora repeated the string of words. The dog rose on his long, graceful legs, but seemed reluctant to obey—even flattening himself down again, whining.

"*Yadhhabu*," she commanded in no uncertain tones, and then the animal whirled to take off, a narrow flash of pale color silhouetted against the darker meadow grass as he ran at full speed toward the pass. Tremaine held his breath, but she'd been right; the enemy couldn't properly gauge the dog's amazing speed, and the two shots fell well-short of their mark.

"Let's go," Tremaine urged, and—the ammo sack slung over his shoulder—he shielded Mora as best he could whilst they dashed toward the building.

Despite her skirts, his wife was almost as fast as he, and the enemy only managed to get off a single shot, as they scrambled though the door and slammed it shut.

"Are you hit?" Tremaine asked, panting.

"No—are you?"

"No." He unslung the ammo sack and tossed it on the wooden table. "We should set-up, back to back."

"*Si*," she agreed, and strode over to yank the curtains down from the windows.

"Stay down," he cautioned.

"It is too far," she countered.

This was true, and the enemy would have to expose themselves on the open meadow if they wanted to advance to a more accurate range. It was a stand-off, at present, but Tremaine knew that the odds weren't in their favor. They were pinned down, and couldn't get to the barn to replenish their ammunition from the stockpile without exposing themselves. They could always use the pebbles from the hearth, but at most it would serve as scatter-shot, and would not be as lethal as musket-balls. Sooner or later, the enemy would realize this and then would probably move-in to use incendiaries; burn the homestead so as to force them out into the open, where they could be picked off at no risk to the attackers. Tremaine knew these tactics well—had employed them many a time, himself. It was a grim scenario, with no defensible strategy—other than the forlorn hope that the enemy was foolish enough to come within range.

Mora was no fool, herself, and obviously knew the odds; he noted that Sahim had not returned, and realized that she must have sent him away to safety—no wonder the poor fellow had been so reluctant to go.

They climbed upon the kitchen table so as to sit, back-to-back, and watch out the windows; having no choice but to await the inevitable.

"I could really use a drink," he teased.

"Quiet," she replied, unamused.

CHAPTER 30

The sun was high in the sky, and Tremaine continued to sit with Mora on the wooden table, his back against hers. There'd been no sign of enemy approach, but this was rather to be expected.

They are waiting until nightfall, Tremaine decided—an easy decision, considering the two corpses in the meadow, currently being feasted upon by the vultures. It would be easier to advance under cover of darkness, and they're in no hurry; they have us pinned, and even if we had any reinforcements coming, they'd only be exposed on the broad meadow, and easy targets for the enemy. There's good reason this place was ideal to run Napoleon's supply trains and—in turn—for the Moroccans' takeover of the same; the geography makes it very easy to control. All in all, the situation is as dire as any I've ever been in.

As was her usual, Mora hadn't said much, but no doubt her thoughts were running along similar lines. Quietly, she said, "*Deus altissimus*."

His gaze still fixed out the window, Tremaine asked, "What does that mean?"

"God is great. It is what the brave man in Algiers said, whenever there was trouble."

"He shouldn't have turned you down."

In a serious tone, she replied, "No—I would not have been good for him. But I think I am good for you."

He drew a long breath. "I'm not good for you, Mora; I spoke of things I shouldn't have, and now we're in this mess."

He could feel her shrug. "If we die, we die."

He could swear she was sincere—she was as rock-steady as they came, and harbored not a single shred of resentment. With all humility, he was moved to say, "Then I will take this opportunity to thank you— I couldn't ask for a better wife. Although you may not think I was worth the trouble, just now."

But she only lifted the pistol slightly. "We will give them trouble, you and me."

"Definitely," he agreed, even as he knew it was hopeless.

After a moment, he continued, "I'm sorry I broke

my promise to you, Mora. I wanted to get the Señora talking, but that's no excuse."

With her usual evenness she replied, "It does not matter, Robert."

"But it does matter," he insisted stubbornly. "It matters to me—I want to ask your forgiveness."

He could sense her surprise. "You are my husband. Of course, I forgive you."

Into the silence, he admitted, "I'm not sure I deserve it."

"You are thinking too much, Robert," she reminded him. "You are a good man."

A bit heavily, he confessed, "I'm not sure the Englishman had the right of it, when he told you this."

She made a derisive sound. "Fah—I am not such a fool as to believe the Englishman in anything. I know this for myself."

He was struck silent, because this, of course, was the pure truth. He realized—realized beyond the shadow of a doubt—that she never would have married him, otherwise; no one would ever force her to do anything, ever again—she'd die, first. And so, she'd married him because she thought he was worthy, and didn't harbor a single regret—even now —mainly because she was not one who second-guessed herself. Indeed, he was fast-coming to the conclusion that she never seemed to give anything a second thought. Whilst he tended to think too much—reliving unhappy memories, and regretting his choices—she lived wholly in the present, and had neither the time nor the patience to dwell on might-have-beens.

I've managed to marry the one woman on earth who didn't think me a dubious prospect, he realized; mainly because her priorities are not like those of other women—in a humbling way, her expectations are, in fact, quite low. It is a shame that I can't spend my life demonstrating to her that I was a better bargain than I seemed, but here we are, and time is growing short.

He tightened his grip on his pistol, as he continued to watch out the window for any signs of movement. She will fight like a tigress to the last breath, he thought; I should do no less.

CHAPTER 31

The long, anxious day had stretched into twilight, and Tremaine mentally tensed for the final confrontation.

Mora had been silent, as they both kept watch, but suddenly she straightened up, and he could hear the relief in her voice. "Sahim returns," she said aloud, and quickly scrambled off the table.

"Hold," he warned, as a scratching could be heard at the door. "It may be a trick."

"No trick," she replied, and opened the door to allow the dog to limp in.

In a panic, he leapt up to pull her back. "Good Lord, Mora—shut the door."

But she only smiled as she disengaged from him, and then went to stand in the open doorway, lifting a hand over her head as though in a signal. "There is no danger, Robert. The enemy is gone."

Bewildered, he stared at her as she shut the door. "Where have they gone?"

"They are dead," she corrected, and snapped her fingers so that the big dog followed her over to the hearth; his head bent low, and his steps slow.

With dawning astonishment, he looked from the woman to the dog. "Sahim has killed them all?"

She shook her head as the dog flopped onto the floor, his long tongue lolling out. "He would have tried, if I had asked, but there would have been too much risk to him."

Making a sympathetic sound, she bent to examine one of the dog's paws, which Tremaine saw was torn and bloody. "If you would bring the bucket, Robert."

With another cautious glance out the windows, he stepped to grab the bucket of water from the hearth, and brought it over to her. "Did he fetch your men back? I didn't hear any gunfire."

"No; I would not lead my men into an ambush," she repeated patiently.

Bewildered, he stared at her. "Then I don't understand; if your men didn't kill them, who did?"

She crouched beside the dog, and tore a strip of cloth from the discarded curtain to dip in the water. "I will tell you a secret, Robert—a secret that my people have known for many, many years. If you wish to gain riches in a foreign place, you must first find out who is their strongman, and then you must pay him, so that he will not fight you." With gentle hands, she wound the bandage around the dog's foot, and tied it off. "It is how such things are done."

Frowning in confusion, he offered, "That's not such a secret, Mora—the British army does the same thing. There are plenty of *Afrancesados* who are being secretly paid to report to the British."

She paused to look up at him almost indulgently. "The *Afrancesados* are not the strongmen here, Robert. The strongmen are the ones who will die for their country, and who don't care who dies along with them."

Realization hit, and he gazed at her in surprise. "The *guerrillas*."

She nodded, and returned to her task. "*Si*; the *guerillas*." With a sigh, she added, "And now, I am beholden to them. It is a shame, but it could not be helped."

In all wonder, he slowly lowered himself into a chair. "You sent Sahim to fetch the *guerrillas*? Lord, he must have covered fifty miles in a single day."

"He is a good dog," she said, and stroked his head fondly.

Still trying to process this near-miracle, Tremaine gazed out into the gathering darkness, hardly daring to believe in such a turnaround. "And they came?"

"It was in their interest to come."

With dawning realization, he shifted his gaze back to her. "That's who gets your stockpile."

"*Si.* They come to collect their payment, from time to time. I leave them alone, they leave me alone." She paused. "But I needed their help, this time. It was no hardship—they would be happy for the chance to kill *Afrancesados,* with no one to know."

Stepping over to the window, he scrutinized the silent mountain face, as the last rays of sunlight reflected off the topmost peak. "Where are they?"

She glanced up at him. "You must be patient, Robert. They will not be seen unless they wish to be seen."

He nodded, knowing this from his own interactions during the war. It would also explain why there'd not been a sound as the enemy was overcome; the *guerrillas* were masters at stealth warfare, and would not have advanced up the mountain openly. It was all very ironic; he'd been thinking it was hopeless—that the mountain's layout made tactical warfare impossible—but he'd forgot that these very mountains had bred warriors who thrived by using completely different tactics.

With the dog's paws bandaged, Mora rose and braced her hands against her back. "We should go to bed now," she said. "I am very tired."

But he only drew her into his arms, resting his

chin on her shoulder. After a moment's hesitation, she wound her arms around him in return, and they stood together for a long moment, in the dim little cabin. "Lord, that was a rough day. Why didn't you tell me you'd sent Sahim for help?"

She pressed her fingers gently into his back. "Because it did not matter, Robert. We would have fought the same, whether they came or not."

"Fair enough." Nevertheless, he suspected she hadn't told him because she didn't want him to overthink things, the way he did—didn't want him to change tactics, if he'd known that rescue might be on its way. She'd the right of it; he'd have probably tried to stall and negotiate so as to spare her life, but that would not have been her preference—her preference was to fight, and fight hard; she'd a reputation to preserve, and if they died, they died.

I don't know as I'll ever truly understand how my wife's mind works, he thought; but at least now I'll have the opportunity to try.

CHAPTER 32

*E*arly the following morning, Tremaine awakened because Sahim had started pacing about the room, clearly agitated.

Out of habit, Tremaine immediately reached for his pistol but then he heard Mora said something to the dog, who quieted.

"My men are hungry," a voice said from outside the window. "Tie-up the dog."

"*Si*," Mora called out. "Bring eggs and chickens from the barn, and I will light the fire."

As he scrambled into his clothes, Tremaine asked in a low voice, "Do we have any concerns?"

"No," she said. "My men are with them—it is the only reason Sahim would allow them to come so close."

And in this, she was right; as Mora began stoking

up the embers in the fire, her men filed in, accompanied by four *guerrillas* and Gerard the gypsy—which was a huge relief to Tremaine, who'd hoped against hope that they'd managed to seize the Romany man before he'd told anyone about the gold.

For his part, Gerard didn't look to be the worse for wear, but instead went to the cupboard to help himself to what remained from yesterday's loaf of bread.

Slightly amused by the man's cavalier attitude, Tremaine decided that he must be well-used to being seized by the various forces who sought his skills, and—due to those very skills—he also knew that it was unlikely anyone would treat him too roughly.

The small room was filled to capacity, as Tremaine assisted Mora with dressing the chickens and putting them on the spit. No one was speaking—not a surprise, perhaps—but Tremaine felt compelled to ask, "Where are the British men?"

One of the *guerrillas*—an older man who was smaller than the others—replied, "They have gone back to their garrison."

This was equal parts a relief and alarming, but Tremaine decided to hold all questions until they'd got the meal underway. In a short time, the men were all eating chicken, bread and eggs—some of them seated on the floor, and sharing the tin plates between them.

As was his habit, Tremaine observed the interactions, and decided that these two groups were not boon companions, but neither were they unfriendly—which made sense, he supposed, if the *guerrillas* were taking a cut from the siphoning operation; Mora was right—there was nothing like a generous payment to smooth-away any resentments.

When Tremaine and Mora joined the others at the table, the older man who'd spoken before wiped his mouth and then offered his hand across the table to Tremaine. "Greetings, *Ingles*. I am Minos."

Tremaine had the immediate sense that this was not, in fact, the man's true name, but he readily took his hand. "Robert Tremaine. I am more than pleased to make your acquaintance, Señor. It was a close-run thing."

Chewing thoughtfully, the smaller man eyed Tremaine for a moment. "You are a surprise to me, Señor."

Hiding his wariness, Tremaine smiled in a friendly fashion. "Oh? And why is this?"

Minos' gaze rested for a moment on Mora. "You woo the Mademoiselle, and promise her riches. You are a braver man than I."

But Mora only shot the man an amused glance, as she continued with her meal. "Fah—there are no riches here, *kafir*. We raise sheep—fine sheep, with thick coats."

"We will give you a cut of the gold," Tremaine said to him immediately, since the reference to riches made it clear that the man had learned of it from Gerard, and Mora's lesson about strongmen was still fresh in his mind. "I am sure we can come to an agreement that will be beneficial to everyone."

Thoughtfully, the *guerrilla* leader nodded. "Yes. I am willing to ally with the British—we must set aside all quarrels."

Interestingly enough, the man looked to Mora for acquiescence—apparently, he was worried about strongmen, too—but she only nodded, unperturbed. "*Si.*"

Lowering his voice, Tremaine glanced at the gypsy man, who had settled in to eat with the others on the floor. "I'm obliged that you managed to intercept Gerard; we can't allow word of the gold to get out."

But Minos only gave him an amused glance from under his brows. "You mistake, Señor; Gerard was coming to find me."

In some surprise, Tremaine stared at him. "He was?"

"*Si.* His tribe and my group, we have long been allies."

Tremaine nodded, but thought—it's a good thing I decided to be honest about the gold mine; the *guerrillas* already knew, and they were no doubt waiting to see how I played it—whether I would be honest with them.

With a contented sigh, Minos sat back in his chair and stretched his legs out. "Gerard has told me something of great interest." He turned his head to address the Romany man. "Will you tell them?"

"You," said Gerard, as he continued eating steadily.

Minos nodded, and dug around in his pocket before pulling out a handful of pebbles, which he slid across the table from his palm, throwing them as though they were dice. "Gerard tells me that these stones are sapphires."

There was a small silence, as Tremaine stared at him in astonishment. Beside him, he could hear Mora suddenly set down her fork.

Incredulous, Tremaine lowered his gaze to the grey pebbles, spread across the table. "*Sapphires*? Are you certain?"

"*Si*," said Gerard, from his position on the floor. "They would need to be cut and polished, of course."

Tremaine reached to lift up a pebble, and turn it between his fingers. "Good *Lord*."

With a chuckle, Minos watched him. "It is very amusing, is it not? To dig for your gold, you must first cast aside the fortune that lies there for the taking."

Blowing out a breath, Tremaine shook his head in

wonder. "We've been using them as hearthstones, and scatter-shot."

"The land holds a fortune."

With a frown, Tremaine turned his attention to Gerard, who was watching his astonishment with a rather smug expression. "Why didn't you tell me?"

The gypsy man shrugged. "You are *gadjo*."

A bit stung by the implied criticism, Tremaine countered, "That may well be, but it's my land, after all."

At this, every eye in the place was suddenly fixed upon him, and he was reminded that he was the odd man out, here; everyone else in the room was a hardened mercenary, including his own wife. Therefore, in a more conciliatory tone, he offered, "But I'm sure we can all come to terms."

Minos nodded, as he clasped his hands across his belly. "*Si*. At first, I think that I will keep Gerard's news to myself—it would be a simple thing to come here at night, and harvest these little stones. But then I think, "Do I wish to cheat the Mademoiselle?""

He glanced over at Mora, who met his gaze with her own, half-amused one. "No," the man continued with a theatrical shudder, "I do not."

"You are wise," Mora remarked.

Minos spread his hands. "And so, we have come to share this news, and discuss what is to be done."

"The British must be informed," Tremaine said in

a firm tone. "I must insist; if there is to be another war, the British are the best able to win it."

"This is—unfortunately—true," Minos agreed. "And so, your two men were sent to the garrison to fetch the Englishman here." Thoughtfully, he nodded to himself. "It is just, in a way. My conscience has plucked at me, because I stole a treasure from him; and so now, I will replace it with another."

"We should all split the proceeds," Tremaine suggested. "The *guerrillas*, the Moroccans, the British —and a portion for the Romanies, too. Everyone will need to work together, if we have any hope of keeping this operation secret, and distributing the gemstones."

"You will raise your sheep," Minos agreed. "I think the *Afrancesados* will send no more suppliers through the pass; they do not wish to fight me in these mountains—they have learned this lesson."

Right," Tremaine agreed. "We should have multiple networks operating; we can smuggle a portion to the port, along with our wool, the gypsies can move them along the rivers, and the *guerrillas* can smuggle them over the pass, and inland."

"Who will handle the money?" asked Mora, who was nothing if not practical.

"The British," Minos said immediately. "They do not know how not to be honest."

At this, everyone chuckled, and Tremaine had to

chuckle, also, even though the merriment was at his expense. It's hard to believe, he thought; but it seems we are holding our own Congress, separate and apart from the one in Vienna but perhaps with equal importance. Of course, the participants here are outlaws instead of diplomats, but I suppose there are plenty who'd say there's not a hair's-breadth of difference, between the two.

CHAPTER 33

The *guerrillas* were loading the stockpile onto their horses—Tremaine was not at all surprised that they wished to stash it away in the hills, before his old commander showed up—and whilst the men worked, their leader had walked out into the meadow, shading his eyes so as to idly watch the birds that flew around the mountain peak.

Reminded of a troubling loose end he needed to mention, Tremaine decided to walk out and join him. The two men stood in silence for a moment, watching the birds, and then Tremaine offered, "They're beautiful, aren't they? I think there's a nest of peregrines, up in the pass."

"Not peregrines," the other man corrected absently. "These are kestrels, instead."

"I stand corrected, then. It seems you know your falcons."

"*Si,*" the other agreed, as he brought his hand down. "I know my falcons."

"I wanted to tell you that there are *Afrancesado* spies, positioned in the town—I wasn't sure if you already knew. I can identify at least two of them; one is the Señora who helps the priest with his duties."

"Ah," the other man replied. "This is of interest. Many thanks, Señor."

"The other is the new banker's clerk—"

"No, no," the *guerrilla* interrupted with a little smile. "Diego will do as I tell him."

There was a small pause. "I don't know as I share your optimism—he seems to be a bit of a weasel."

But his companion shrugged slightly. "Do not worry; I will speak with him—I know him well. He was going to marry a Grandee and live a life of ease, and so now he is bitter and will leap at the chance, if anyone promises him a life of riches and importance." He paused, and sighed. "Diego is not an evil man, but he is weak—weak and bitter that his life did not turn out as he'd wished."

Tremaine smiled a bit grimly. "Aren't we all."

But his joking response was met with a full measure of seriousness, as the older man lifted his gaze to meet Tremaine's. "You must not be bitter, *Ingles*; it will eat up your soul. Instead, you must do as *El Buen Señor* asks, and do not think that you know better how to run the world."

A bit taken aback, Tremaine managed to nod. "I suppose that's true. And believe it or not, my wife has given me very similar advice."

With a grimace, Minos returned his gaze to the mountains. "I do not think she spends much time at prayer, that one. I could tell you tales—but you are her husband, and so I choose not to."

But Tremaine found that he felt compelled to defend his unlikely wife. "We can't know how any of us would react, if we'd lived the life she has—if we'd survived what she had to survive."

The other man lowered his head in concession. "It makes our own worries look not so very terrible, does it not?"

"Yes. And speaking of such, I can't thank you enough. Not only did you save our lives, you have been very generous; I know it must rankle to share Spanish treasure."

But the *guerrilla* only shrugged. "It was in my interest, *Ingles*. There is a young Señora who would flay me alive if I did not help the British—she is married to such a one."

Tremaine smiled. "That doesn't mean I can't be grateful, all the same. Anytime I can return the favor, you have only to ask."

The other man nodded, as they turned to retrace

their steps to the homestead. "Come, then; we will toast our new alliance."

But Tremaine shook his head. "I'm not allowed to drink anymore; I've my own Señora who would flay me alive."

The older man chuckled. "Then I will toast alone—I will toast all the Señoras who spur us to be better men, whether we are willing or not."

"God bless them all," Tremaine agreed.

CHAPTER 34

"We'll have to buy more sheep," Tremaine teased Mora. "Lots and lots of stupid sheep."

It was evening, and they were lying in bed—there was no privacy to be had, with all the men underfoot—and so they'd retreated to the bedroom to discuss the surprising events of the day.

"If I must tend sheep, I will tend sheep," she replied stoically.

"Not the best use of your skills, perhaps, but in the end, it will be well-worth it. Not only will the Knights be grateful, you may actually live a bit longer."

"This is true," she agreed. "And so, I will do it."

The listened to the muffled tones of the men,

speaking to each other in the next room, and then Mora observed in a practical tone, "We will need more chickens, too. The *Españoles* have eaten almost all of them."

With a chuckle, he drew her close, so that her head rested against his shoulder. "I'll build a chicken coop, next to the barn. And I'd like to set about shoring-up this place, so that the building is more solid—I should add another room anyway, for when those little girls come along. But first things first; we'll need at least one more fireplace or you're going to freeze, if we stay here for the winter."

"If you wish," she replied, as though it meant little to her, either way.

Thinking about this, he ventured, "We could always winter someplace warmer, if you'd like—and come up after the thaw. I imagine the operation will have to cease during the winter, anyway."

"No," she said simply. "I like it here."

"You like who you are, when you are here," he offered, remembering what she'd once said.

"*Sí*."

"I like who I am, too," he confessed. "It's strange; this feels rather like home to me—all the good parts of home, without any of the bad parts. Although I suppose that was a bad part in the meadow, yesterday—wouldn't want to have to do that again."

"That was a good part," she said.

He couldn't help but chuckle. "No better illustration, of how you and I are different."

Her breast rose and fell. "Perhaps."

Thoughtfully, he added, "We may be very different, but in a lot of ways we're very similar."

"You are thinking too much, Robert," she warned.

"I'll stop," he agreed. "And I will point out that if we're going to winter here, I may have to fashion some leather booties for Sahim—I don't think he'll do well in the snow."

"You must not spoil him, Robert."

"On the contrary, I will spoil him as much as I like."

She sighed. "The English are so strange; they treat their dogs like children, instead of like workers."

"Or weapons," he added.

"Or weapons," she agreed, without a shred of self-consciousness.

"Speaking of such, I don't think the Englishman likes him much; best tie Sahim outside, when he arrives."

"No, Robert," she explained patiently. "It is because the Englishman does not like him that Sahim will stay in the room."

"Ah—I stand corrected."

They lay in silence for a few minutes, whilst

Tremaine contemplated the spymaster's anticipated reaction to their good news. No need to wait for the gold mine to be up and producing; instead, a fortune was readily available—and more easily smuggled to where it would be needed.

This whole turn of events was nothing short of miraculous, and never would have come to pass, save for the happenstance of three completely unconnected things coming together; his own background in mining, his dogged determination to redeem himself, and a clever gypsy's visit to the site—which was a direct result of the first two things. It did give one pause; maybe the old *guerrilla* had the right of it —about leaving things in the hands of *El Buen Señor*, who was better at running the world than he could ever be.

In any case, one way or another it had all worked out just as he'd hoped. Well—not exactly; it was more as though he'd been swept along in a series of tumultuous events, trying to stay afloat amidst all the twists and turns. And it had not escaped his notice that—although his aim had been first and foremost to redeem himself—as soon as he'd started to focus on something other than his own problems, his mind seemed to quieten. It was very similar, he suspected, to what had happened to Mora, when she'd started to focus on helping the Knights, rather than pursuing a vicious revenge against all who'd harmed her.

He didn't dare mention it, else she'd tell him he was thinking too much again, and so—bringing to mind Mora's advice on that subject—he gathered her into his arms and began to nuzzle her neck; she had her own, distinct scent—it made him think of sun-warmed skin, and the timeless desert. "Can we be quiet enough, do you think?"

"I am always quiet," she said, as she willingly ran her hands up his chest. "It is you, who must be quiet."

But Sahim suddenly took an interest—in the way dogs tended to do—and rested his head on the bed, watching them closely.

Tremaine paused to chuckle. "Shall I put him out?"

"No—he will only be worse, if he is separated from me."

"Not to mention that everyone is terrified of him."

"You are not, though," she observed with a hint of wonder. "You never were."

"No," Tremaine agreed. He reached to run a hand across the dog's head, where it rested on the bed, and the gesture evoked a brief wag of the animal's tail. "He's a good fellow—no one else I'd rather have at my back, than Sahim—and Sahim's mistress."

Twining her arms around his neck, she sighed. "This is a very fine compliment, Robert."

He contemplated the amusing fact that his wife would appreciate a compliment about her battle-prowess more than she would one about her appearance, but knew better than to make a remark; instead, he began to kiss her in earnest, carefully positioning his foot so as to keep the dog away.

Made in the USA
Columbia, SC
28 July 2024